Laugh Out Loud

JAMES PATTERSON is the internationally bestselling author of the highly praised Middle School books, *Homeroom Diaries*, *Kenny Wright: Superhero*, *Word of Mouse*, *Pottymouth and Stoopid*, *Laugh Out Loud* and the I Funny, Jacky Ha-Ha, Treasure Hunters, House of Robots, Confessions, Maximum Ride, Witch & Wizard and Daniel X series. James Patterson books have sold more than 365 million copies worldwide, making him one of the biggest-selling authors of all time. He lives in Florida.

HOW I SURVIVED BULLIES, BROCCOLI, AND SNAKE HILL

(with Chris Tebbetts)

I'm excited for a fun summer at camp—until I find out it's a summer *school* camp. There's no fun and games here, just a whole lotta trouble!

ULTIMATE SHOWDOWN

(with Julia Bergen)

Who would have thought that we—Rafe and Georgia—would ever agree on anything? That's right—we're writing a book together. And the best part? We want you to be part of the fun too!

SAVE RAFE!

(with Chris Tebbetts)

I'm in worse trouble than ever! I need to survive a gut-bustingly impossible outdoor excursion so I can return to school next year. But will I get through it in one piece?

JUST MY ROTTEN LUCK

(with Chris Tebbetts)

I'm heading back to the place it all began: Hills Village Middle School, but only if I take "special" classes...If that wasn't bad enough, when I somehow land a place on the school football team, I find myself playing alongside none other than the biggest bully in school, Miller the Killer!

DOG'S BEST FRIEND

(with Chris Tebbetts)

It's a dog-eat-dog world. When I started my own dog-walking empire, I didn't think it could go so horribly wrong! Somehow, I always seem to end up in deep doo-doo...

ESCAPE TO AUSTRALIA
(with Martin Chatterton)
I just won an all-expenses-paid trip of a lifetime to Australia. But here's the bad news: I MIGHT NOT MAKE IT OUT ALIVE!

The I FUNNY Series

I FUNNY
(with Chris Grabenstein)
Join Jamie Grimm at middle school where he's on an unforgettable mission to win the Planet's Funniest Kid Comic Contest. Dealing with the school bully (who he also happens to live with) and coping with a disability are no trouble for Jamie when he has laughter on his side.

I EVEN FUNNIER
(with Chris Grabenstein)
Heading to the national semi-finals, Jamie's one step closer to achieving his dream! But will a sudden family health scare put his ambitions on hold?

I TOTALLY FUNNIEST
(with Chris Grabenstein)
Jamie's heading to Hollywood for his biggest challenge yet. There's only the small matter of the national finals and eight other laugh-a-minute competitors between him and the trophy—oh, and a hurricane!

I FUNNY TV
(with Chris Grabenstein)
Jamie has achieved his dream of becoming the Planet's Funniest Kid Comic, and now the sky's the limit! Enter a couple of TV executives with an offer for Jamie to star in his very own show...

SCHOOL OF LAUGHS
(with Chris Grabenstein)
Jamie has a national contest trophy and a TV show
under his belt, but teaching other kids how to be funny is
the toughest gig that he has ever had. And if he fails, his
school library will be shut down for good!

TREASURE HUNTERS
(with Chris Grabenstein)
The Kidds are not your normal family, traveling the world on
crazy adventures to recover lost treasure. But when their parents
disappear, Bick and his brother and sisters are thrown into the
biggest (and most dangerous) treasure hunt of their lives. Evil
pirates, tough guys and gangsters stand in their way, but can
they work together to find their mom and dad?

DANGER DOWN THE NILE
(with Chris Grabenstein)
Bick, Beck, Storm and Tommy are navigating their way
down the Nile, from a hot and dusty Cairo to deep dark
jungles, past some seriously bad guys along the way.

SECRET OF THE FORBIDDEN CITY
(with Chris Grabenstein)
The Kidds are desperately trying to secure the ancient
Chinese artefact that will buy their mother's freedom from
kidnapping pirates.

PERIL AT THE TOP OF THE WORLD

(with Chris Grabenstein)

When the biggest heist in history takes place in Moscow, the Kidds rush in to save the day—but instead, they're accused of being the thieves themselves!

QUEST FOR THE CITY OF GOLD

(with Chris Grabenstein)

When Storm is kidnapped, the Kidds must locate the lost Incan City of Paititi...before the bad guys find it first.

HOUSE OF ROBOTS

(with Chris Grabenstein)

Sammy is just your average kid...except he lives in a house full of robots! Most of the time it's pretty cool. But then there's E, the worst robot ever. He's a know-it-all, thinks he's Sammy's brother, AND he's about to go to the same school! Come see if Sammy *ever* manages to make any friends with a loser robot tagging along...

ROBOTS GO WILD!

(with Chris Grabenstein)

Sammy and E are finally making some friends at school. But disaster strikes when E malfunctions just in time to be upstaged by the super-cool new robot on the block.

ROBOT REVOLUTION
(with Chris Grabenstein)
When Sammy's inventor mom becomes distracted by a
top-secret project, the robots soon begin to fall into disrepair.
Cue a robot revolution!

THE
JACKY HA-HA
SERIES

JACKY HA-HA
(with Chris Grabenstein)
With her irresistable urge to tell a joke in every
situation—even when she really shouldn't—twelve-year-old
Jacky Ha-Ha loves to make people laugh. And cracking wise
helps distract her from thinking about not-so-funny things
in her life, like her mom serving in a dangerous, faraway
war, and a dad who's hardly ever home.

MY LIFE IS A JOKE
(with Chris Grabenstein)
It's summertime on the shore, and for Jacky Hart it's
all about her starring role in the boardwalk's biggest
blockbuster!

KENNY WRIGHT: SUPERHERO

(with Chris Tebbetts)
Kenny is the life-saving, world-famous superhero otherwise known as Stainlezz Steel. He's taken down General Zod twice, beaten Darth Vader at chess... and lives with his grandma. Okay, sometimes he gets a bit carried away. But G-ma really does need his help now—and he's going to have to be a superhero to save the day.

WORD of MOUSE

(with Chris Grabenstein)
Raised in a laboratory, Isaiah is extremely smart, but scared of everything. One day, he manages to escape and is forced to leave his family behind. All alone now, Isaiah has to quickly learn to survive in the dangerous outdoors.

Pottymouth and Stoopid

(with Chris Grabenstein)
David and his best friend Michael were tagged with awful nicknames in preschool. Fast-forward to seventh grade: "Pottymouth" and "Stoopid" are still stuck with the names. So how do they go about changing everyone's minds? By turning their misery into megastardom on TV, of course!

Laugh Out Loud

James Patterson
and Chris Grabenstein

Illustrated by Jeff Ebbeler

1 3 5 7 9 10 8 6 4 2

Young Arrow
20 Vauxhall Bridge Road
London SW1V 2SA

Young Arrow is part of the Penguin Random House group of
companies whose addresses can be found at
global.penguinrandomhouse.com

 Penguin
Random House
UK

First published by Young Arrow in 2017
This edition published in paperback by Young Arrow in 2018

www.penguin.co.uk

A CIP catalogue record for this book is available
from the British Library

ISBN 9781784758493

For Aubrey Poole and Jenny Bak.

—JP

For all the teachers who make reading fun!

—CG

Chapter 1

Dream Big!

Hi, my name is Jimmy and you're reading one of my books!

Well, actually, it's *your* book. Or the library's. Or maybe it's your friend's or your cousin's or your sister's and they lent it to you, which means they're sort of like a library (which is totally awesome, by the way).

The point is, I, Jimmy, published this book. That's right. I made it at my own book-making company called...ta-da: JIMMY!

1

I have to tell you: seeing that JIMMY logo on the cover of this book is pretty cool.

You want to go back and look at it again?

Go ahead. I'll wait.

(While you're checking it out, I'll hum something from *Echo* by Pam Muñoz Ryan, one of my favorite books about the power of music!)

You're back? Great!

For me, that little JIMMY thingy is my dream come true.

I don't know this for sure, but I think the most important thing in the world is for kids to have dreams.

What's yours?

You do dream, don't you? And not just when you're sleeping. I'm talking about a BIG, wide-awake, I'll-do-whatever-it-takes-to-make-it-happen kind of dream. Something like winning the Olympics, finding the cure for a scary disease, stopping your little brother from gumming up the Xbox controller with peanut butter again, or running your own book company.

Fact is that ever since I was a little kid (yeah, yeah—soooo long ago, right?) I've loved books.

3

You ever hear that saying, "Do what you love, love what you do"? Well, that's exactly why I wanted to start my own book company.

I know how crazy that sounds. Laugh-out-loud nutso. At least that's what all the grown-ups in my life kept telling me.

"That sounds crazy," said my uncle Herman.

"Laugh-out-loud nutso," added aunt Irene.

"Run a book company? You?" said this bald guy named Jeff. "You're just a middle schooler! You won't stand a chance, kid. I'll crush you like a cockroach—just like I crushed all the other, *older* cockroaches who came before you!"

(Jeff, I think, runs his own book company.)

But like I said, a kid has to have a dream before any of his dreams can come true.

So here's how everything happened; how an ordinary kid like me got his own publishing company. It's so exciting, I could write a book about it.

So guess what?

I did!

Chapter 2

My Marvelous Visitors

Okay, here's how my book company got started.

Late one summer night, I went walking with my dog, Quixote, which, by the way is pronounced KEY-HO-TAY. That's right. I named him after the lead character from the classic Spanish novel *The Ingenious Gentleman Don Quixote of La Mancha* by Miguel de Cervantes Saavedra. (Don't ask me how to pronounce *his* last name. I'm still trying to learn how to say *¿Dónde está el baño?*) It's all about this guy who is an epic dreamer and fights windmills. He's kind of a weird dude.

Anyway, we weren't too far from our house

in San Jose, California, and I was reading *The Marvels* by Brian Selznick.

Yep. I love books so much I can walk and read at the same time.

Unless there is an open manhole. Or a curb. Curbs are tough.

Anyway, have you read *The Marvels*? The first half is told completely in pencil drawings: Crashing waves are about to sink the *Kraken,* a whaling ship, where our hero, Billy Marvel, is putting on a show for the sailors.

Man, I was totally lost in Mr. Selznick's amazing tale.

So lost, I didn't notice the creepy clump of trees Quixote and I had just wandered into.

We kept walking deeper and deeper into the darkness, because I kept falling deeper and deeper into Brian Selznick's swirling tale of adventure.

Hey, when I'm into a book, I crawl in all the way!

On the illustrated pages, lightning flashed and thunder boomed. Billy was about to be swept overboard as the ship sank!

I could hear the wooden beams of the *Kraken* creaking and groaning as the waves pounded its sides.

Splinters and wood chips showered down all around me.

(Yeah, actual wood stuff falling from the sky was a little weird. Even for a guy who totally lives in his imagination like me.)

Then the crackling and snapping grew louder. It sounded like trees were exploding all around me! Seconds later, the splintering sounds were blasted away by the humongous rumbling THWUMP and WARBLE of unearthly engines.

The darkness was replaced by a dusty shaft of bright white light.

I finally looked up from my book. Quixote

looked up, too. Then he whimpered and tucked his tail between his legs.

Because the two of us were standing right where the hovering alien spaceship wanted to land.

Chapter 3

Greetings, People Not of Earth

The flying saucer snapped off a few more branches as it completed its slow descent to the ground and settled with a soft, airy KOOSH!

Quixote whined and grumbled. I think he wanted to go home.

Not me. I wanted to see who (or what) was inside the spaceship!

A side door ZHURRR-WHOOSHed open. A gangplank slid forward. And the parade started! Just about every creature from every space story ever told was crammed on board that one ship!

It was like a minivan hauling the all-star soccer team from all the stars.

Some I recognized from movies and TV. Others were from books, like Mrs. Whatsit from Madeleine L'Engle's *A Wrinkle in Time* and Hilo from *The Boy Who Crashed to Earth* by Judd Winick.

They were all extremely friendly, so we spent the night sitting around, talking.

The space creatures all thought some of the things we earthlings had were weird. Like spray cheese in a can. And silly string in a can. And joke-store springy snakes that jump out of cans.

Yes, they were seriously hung up on cans. Maybe because they spend so much time sealed up inside spaceships.

And farts. None of them understood farts.

"Is this some kind of internal gas-powered jet propulsion you employ after eating beans?" they wondered.

That's when a guy with a bubble-brain head and ginormous bug eyes spoke up. I wasn't exactly sure what movie or book he came from. Probably one like *The War of the Worlds* by H. G. Wells where the aliens aren't all that cute and cuddly.

"We have a very important message for the planet Earth," the alien said in a mechanical voice (he sounded like he ate computer chips for lunch every day). "Extremely, enormously, urgently important."

Prepare to receive vital data, earthling.

I'm all ears. And you're all eyes.

Yep, this was first contact, the very first official words humans had ever received from outer space, and I was going to be the human doing all the receiving!

Roughly translated, what the big head basically said was "Your planet is in really, really, really deep doo-doo."

(I can't repeat the actual words the spaceman used. Moms and teachers don't like that kind of language. If I used the actual words, they wouldn't let kids read this book, and if that happened, you'd miss a really cool story.)

"The people of earth," the space ambassador continued, "must read more, and learn more, and *think* a whole lot more. Or else."

I gulped a little. Quixote whimpered again.

"You must assist your fellow earthlings in this effort!" said another one of the aliens. "You must open a book company, Jimmy!"

"Do this you must," added Yoda.

"Or else," said Marvin the Martian.

And he was aiming his ray gun straight at me!

Chapter 4

Meanwhile, Back in Reality...

Okay, okay, okay.

You've probably already figured out that this wasn't how JIMMY Books got started. It wasn't because aliens landed in California and told me I had to do it to save the planet.

But it shows you just how much I love stories.

Love, love, *love* 'em!

You also know that I did, eventually, start JIMMY Books. I mean, you're reading a JIMMY Book, right? If I'd never started the company we wouldn't be having this conversation.

15

So here's how it really happened. The truth. You could shelve this next bit in the nonfiction section because it's the real deal. Except for where I might exaggerate. Or make up another story for the fun of it. But even then it's still mostly true.

Like I said before all those aliens landed, everyone should have a dream. Maybe a couple of dreams. My dream was to start an amazing book company while I was still a kid. That's right. This wasn't going to be one of those "when I grow up, I wanna" kind of dreams they make you write about in middle school essays.

Nope. I wanted to create a book company for kids, by kids, and of kids. That was my dream.

The girl who lived next door? She dreamed about leaving her room and playing with all the kids she watched out her window every day.

Her name was Madison. She was severely asthmatic and had a bunch of other health problems with complicated names that sound weirder than the alien word for "deep doo-doo."

The grown-ups all called my next-door neighbor "sickly."

I just called her Maddie.

I hope you like half these books. Because if I have to carry them all home, they'll crack my back.

Maddie was the reason I always carried twice as many library books in my backpack as I could ever read before they were due. Half were for me, half were for her.

The librarian at school, Ms. Nicole Sprenkle, was cool about it, too. Hey, she might've loved books even more than me—if that's mathematically possible.

Whenever I visited Maddie I had to wear a sterile mask. I didn't mind. I just pretended I was a doctor or a bank robber or a test pilot flying at the speed of sound.

"How'd you like to be stranded in a blizzard at the Washington, DC, airport?" I asked Maddie, handing her a copy of Kate Messner's *Capture the Flag*.

She sort of shrugged. "I guess it would be okay."

"Okay?" I said. "Why, before long, I bet you'd be tracking down the despicable thieves who just stole the two-hundred-year-old flag that flew over Fort McHenry and inspired Francis Scott Key to write 'The Star-Spangled Banner.' Too bad none of the grown-ups will listen to you or your friends after you present your evidence about what the bad guys are up to."

Maddie practically ripped the book out of my hands and dove right in.

It made her dream come true. For 240 pages, she was out of her room and on an action-packed adventure in Washington, DC, that included a thrilling trip along airport baggage conveyor belts!

Yep. Books can be better than an amusement park. They'll take you on all sorts of wild rides. And you don't have to worry about long lines or finding a place to park.

That night, Maddie called me. She'd already finished *Capture the Flag*.

"Jimmy?" she said.

"Yeah?"

"Give me another book. Please?"

Chapter 5

Working on a Dream

I figured there were tons of kids just like Maddie all over the world.

Not that they were sick all the time. But they were hungry—maybe even starving—for fun and exciting books.

That meant I would need to make lots and lots of books. But how could I pull it off? Don't forget, I was just a kid. Still am. But being a kid has its advantages. For one thing, we eat a lot of delicious sugary snacks. Sugar will keep your mind buzzing.

Plus, kids wake up earlier than adults. That's why they invented cartoons, which we watch while eating sugary cereal. Talk about a mental buzz.

After brainstorming for weeks, it was time to start putting my thoughts down on paper. I drew sketches whenever and wherever I could of what I wanted my book company to look like.

By the way, drawing while walking gets easier with practice.

Still, I don't recommend doing it while riding a bike or skateboarding. You bump into stuff. Stuff like fire hydrants and lamp poles.

I was obsessed.

All the kids at school were totally into my dream, too.

"I want to work at your book company!" said my good friend Chris Grabbetts. "I like writing."

"You mean you have fun making up stories, too?"

"Sometimes. But mostly, I like *writing*. Especially cursive. I'm thinking about taking up calligraphy, except I don't know how to spell it." Like always, Chris was joking around.

"Instead of freight elevators, you need a Ferris wheel to move books from one floor to the other," suggested my bud Raphael Katchadopoulos, whom everybody calls Rafe. He's pretty good with markers and a sketchpad so he doodled a quick visual. I love, love, loved it.

"You also need a bowling alley," said Chris.

I raised both eyebrows. "A bowling alley?"

He shrugged. "I like to bowl."

"I'll put a lane over here near the ping-pong and foosball tables," said Rafe, his pen scribbling across the page.

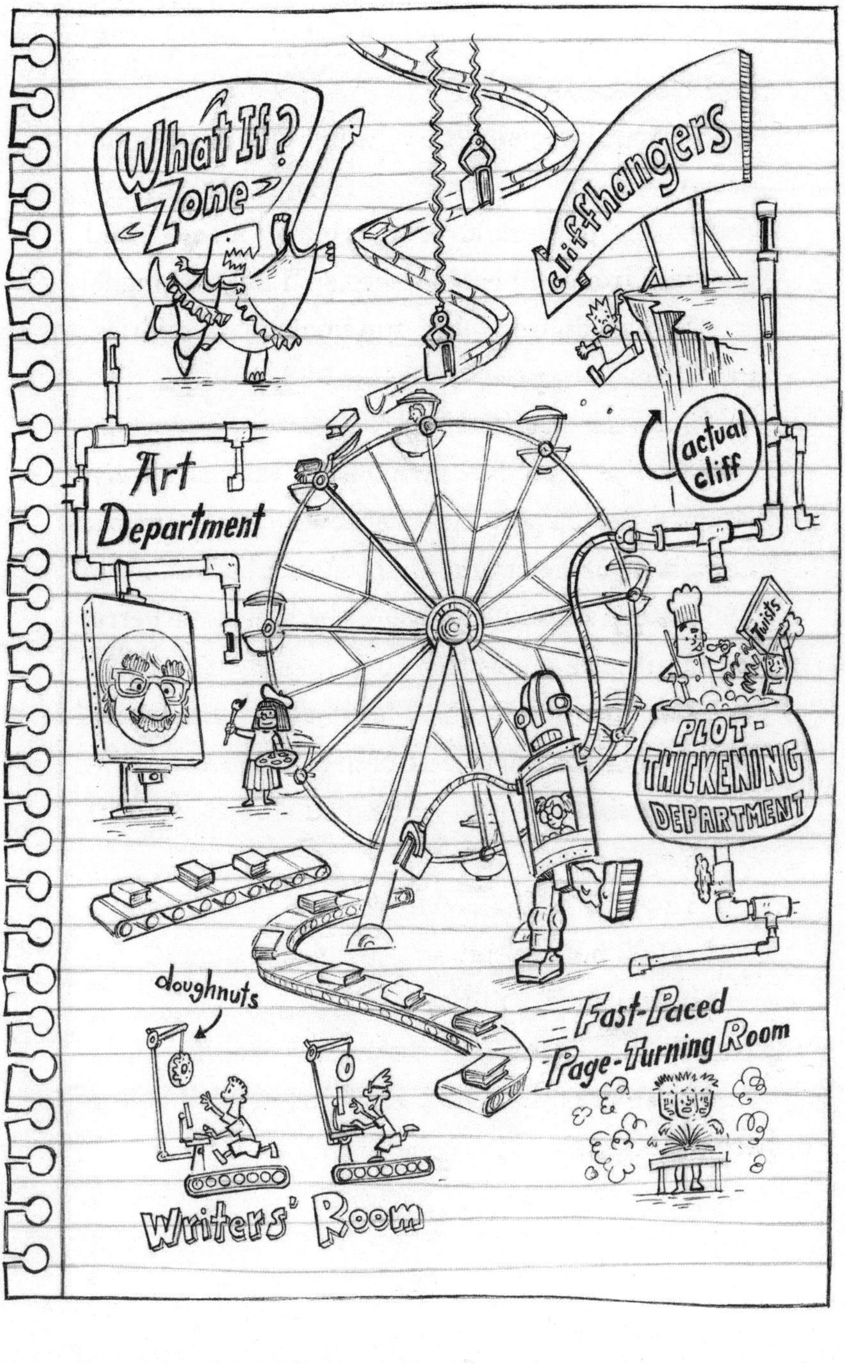

What If? Zone
Cliffhangers
actual cliff
Art Department
Twists
PLOT-THICKENING DEPARTMENT
doughnuts
Fast-Paced Page-Turning Room
Writers' Room

"You need a bouncy house," said Maxine Peterman, another great pal of mine. "A place where employees can eat and goof off on their lunch break."

"But won't all that bouncing up and down make people lose their lunch?" worried Chris.

"Even better," said Maxine with a shrug. "Projectile vomit is always fun."

With everybody's awesome ideas, my dream factory was inching closer and closer to becoming a reality. At the end of the month, I had an actual blueprint—mostly because I drew it with a blue ballpoint pen.

Yep, everybody at school was super excited about my big idea.

My parents?

Not so much.

Chapter 6

Meet the 'Rents

So this is Mom and Dad.

These people totally take the merry out of Christmas.

Dad's a big-time CPA, a certified public accountant. That means he crunches numbers for other people and does their taxes for them. Mom is a hotshot lawyer. The kind that handles tax stuff. I sometimes wonder if Mom and Dad met on April fifteenth. You know—tax day.

Mom never goes to court or does anything dramatic like, say, the awesome Atticus Finch in *To Kill a Mockingbird*. Instead of drama and excitement, my parents both have huge, boxy briefcases filled with paper. Not books. Paper. Reams and reams of it. Dad's papers are covered in lines, grids, graphs, and numbers. Mom's have Post-it notes sticking out between the pages.

You know how most grown-ups work nine to five? My mom and dad work five to nine. That's right. They head to their offices at 5 a.m. and don't come home until 9 p.m., just in time to ask me if I finished my homework and say a quick good night.

I sometimes wondered if I was actually an orphan, like some of my favorite characters in books. Harry Potter. Anne Shirley. Oliver Twist. Cinderella.

In fact, I had a hunch that my real parents had

been eaten by an angry rhinoceros so the couple I called my mother and father were actually my aunt Sponge and uncle Spiker. I kept waiting for an enormous enchanted orange to grow on a barren orange tree in our backyard so I could fly in it like a hot-air balloon, meet a bunch of friendly talking bugs, and set sail for New York City!

But then I realized, that wasn't my story. It was *James and the Giant Peach* by Roald Dahl—I just changed the fruit because I'd had orange juice for breakfast.

Yep, there are a lot of orphans in books. Comic books, too. Batman, Superman, Spider-Man, the Hulk, Daredevil, Robin, Aquagirl—all those super-heroes without any 'rents.

Sometimes, that's how I felt.

Minus the X-ray vision or web-slinging.

My superpower?

Reading!

Chapter 7

Sharing My Dream

Late one night, after Mom and Dad had both been home for like thirty minutes, I decided to show them my dream on paper.

Actually, it was more like a dream on papers. I kept having more and more great ideas. So I taped all the different sketches together in one ginormous quilt, which I rolled up and carried into the dining room.

It was maybe ten o'clock. They were both sitting at the table, not eating. Cardboard and Styrofoam cartons of cold takeout food sat next to their stacks of papers.

I tiptoed into the room with my tube of taped-together sketches.

"Mom? Dad?" I said. "I want to show you something."

"Is it your homework?" asked Dad. "Because it's tax season, Jimmy, and I really need to finish these forms for Ferguson Fine Furniture before I can even look at your algebra equations."

"I can't help you, either," said Mom. "I need to familiarize myself with the particulars of this legal brief. The tax issues are quite complex."

"Well, Mom," I said with a flourish, "since you need to study a brief, I'll be *brief*, too. Ta-da!"

I unfurled my grand schematic.

Mom and Dad stared at my humongous sheet of factory plans. Then they blinked.

Finally, Dad said, "Is that an amusement park you want to visit, Jimmy? Because I don't get any vacation time until after April fifteenth..."

"It looks more like a floor plan," said Mom.

"Exactly," I said eagerly. "It's the floor plan for a kids' book company run by kids that makes books for other kids."

More staring and blinking.

"Why?" asked Mom.

"Because kids like Maddie next door need books."

"Is that a Ferris wheel?" asked Dad.

"Yep."

"Why?"

"It's way cooler than a freight elevator."

"Interesting," said Dad. Then he went back to his ledger sheets.

Mom went back to her legal briefs.

"It's my dream!" I told them.

"Next time," added Dad, "don't waste so much paper and tape, Jimmy. Paper and tape are not tax-deductible expenses for a boy your age."

I rolled up my sketches and headed back to my bedroom.

I don't think my mother and father have dreams anymore. I think they rolled them up and tucked them away when they were kids.

Then they forgot where they hid them.

Chapter 8

Back to School

As you probably already guessed, I wasn't going to let my parents' lack of enthusiasm crush my dream.

It's like they say in James Dashner's *The Maze Runner* (a very cool book, btw): "We can't give up. Ever." (And then they say, "Run! Through the maze! Run!")

Plus, all my friends at school were still stoked about making my by-kids/for-kids book company happen.

"You're going to need an art department," said Rafe.

"I know!" I told him. "And I'm going to need you to run it!"

He grinned. "My point exactly."

My friend Steve Bowman was already thinking about our first film projects.

"We'll make movies," said Steve. "A lot of movies start as books."

"Hey, Jimmy?" My next-door neighbor's little brother, Sammy, came charging up the hall. "Maddie needs another book. Like now. She's stuck inside for the rest of the month. The pollen count is too high."

"Here you go." I reached into my locker and pulled out my personal, dog-eared copy of one of my all-time faves: *A Week in the Woods* by Andrew Clements. When she cracked open the cover, Maddie could go snowshoeing, go camping, and get totally lost in the woods.

"Thanks!" said Maddie's little brother. "And Jimmy?"

"Yeah?"

"Hurry up and start your book company, already!"

Yep, everybody at school was excited about my book company, even though it wasn't much more than an idea and bunch of sketches. Wait. Rewind. Check that.

All the *kids* at school were excited.

The grown-ups? Most of them were, more or less, in my parents' camp.

"Not gonna happen, kid," said Bob the janitor. Then he showed me his faded drawings for a baseball stadium on the moon.

"I drew this back when I was in middle school. Never could figure out how to stop every base hit from turning into a home run, what with there being no atmosphere on the moon to slow down the ball and that whole 'five-sixths of earth's gravity' thing. Guess I wasted my time dreaming this baby up, huh?"

Then there was Mr. Quackenberry.

Chapter 9

The World According to Quackenberry

Mr. Quackenberry taught history and loved telling us about "the most colossal, most stupendous, and hugest failures in history."

"Big ideas lead to nothing but big disappointment!" was his catchphrase.

Then he'd tell us about the *Titanic*. The giant cruise ship that sank on its first voyage.

Or how a Mars orbiter was messed up because NASA used the metric system for measurements while the dudes building it used the English system of yards and feet.

"And need I remind you children of the Edsel?" Mr. Quackenberry would say with delight. "Oh, the Edsel! In 1959, Henry Ford made exactly the wrong car and named it after his son, Edsel B. Ford. It turned into a two-hundred-and-fifty-million-dollar mistake. In today's dollars, that would be one point eight five billion!"

Mr. Quackenberry was always telling us "the timeline of history is littered with the shards of shattered dreams." Then he'd giggle with glee.

"Dreams are for fools, children! All dreams do is ruin a good night's sleep and make you believe you could actually be a contestant on *Jeopardy!* when you know they'll never even write you back no matter how many cards you send in and how well you do when you play against the TV!"

I'd heard enough.

"One day," I said defiantly, "I'm going to make my dream come true! I'm going to open a book company! You'll see."

Mr. Quackenberry smirked. "Right. It'll never happen, kid."

I didn't mind.

Mr. Quackenberry was just one more grown-up I'd have to prove wrong!

Chapter 10

Dream Job

Luckily, there was one adult at school who didn't laugh out loud at my dream. Ms. Sprenkle.

"My dream came true, Jimmy," she told me. "Yours can, too."

"That's awesome!" I said. "So what was your dream?"

She spread her arms open wide.

"This! To be a librarian. To spend my days surrounded by great stories and amazing facts that I can share with the world. Just think about it, Jimmy—there are incredible adventures sitting on every single shelf in this room. All of them just waiting for you or me or somebody to crack them open, dive in, and make the action begin again."

The way she said it, I could see it!

The library. The most crowded room in any school!

"I'd like to add a few new characters to your world," I told Ms. Sprenkle. "When I start making books, I want to make characters that'll leap off the page!"

"There's always room for more, Jimmy. A book may only be an inch or two thick, but inside, you could find a cast of thousands. You can also meet famous people from the past, travel to distant lands, or learn how to build your own robot. I think author Neil Gaiman said it best: 'A book is a dream you can hold in your hand!'"

"So you don't think I'm nutso for wanting to start my own book company?"

"Nutso for creating more dreams for people to hold in their hands? Impossible. You love reading, right?"

"You bet!"

"And telling stories?"

"I love, love, *love* that."

"Well, Jimmy, here's my advice, for what it's worth: Do what you love and you'll never have to work a day in your life."

"You mean I won't need to get a job, like Mom and Dad?"

"No. What I mean is if you love your job, work will never seem like *work*. Just don't give up trying to do what you really want to do. 'Where there is love and inspiration, I don't think you can go wrong.'"

"Wow. That's a pretty inspirational slogan, Ms. Sprenkle."

"Thank you, but I can't take credit for it. The legendary jazz singer Ella Fitzgerald said it first. This library also has a lot of books filled with famous quotations."

So I had one grown-up (and Ella Fitzgerald) on my side.

Maybe that would be all I needed to make my dream come true!

Chapter 11

Ideas Take Flight

One day after school, my friends and I were hanging out at our favorite coffee shop in San Jose.

Not that any of us drink coffee. We prefer those slushy drinks with all the whipped cream and squiggly caramel sauce on top.

"You can't let Mr. Quackenberry demoralize you," said my brainiac friend Pierce, who is a total techno geek. His dad and mom are both Silicon Valley engineers—they design and build cool stuff. Pierce probably could be one, too. He's already built six robots by snapping together junked computers and spare electronic parts. "However, you do need to formulate a workable production plan if you truly hope to one day turn your aspiration into a practical reality."

"What?" (I sometimes wish I had one of those visiting aliens I imagined to help me translate what Pierce says.)

"If you're going to make books," asked Maxine, "what do you need first, Jimmy?"

"Story ideas," I told her. "Ideas are where everything starts. Good thing I have a folder full of 'em. It's six inches thick."

Then I told my friends this idea I had about a group of kids who could fly.

"Like in *Peter Pan*?" said Chris.

"Not exactly. These would be ordinary kids, except they have wings."

"Huh?" said Steve.

"They're genetic mutants who escaped from a mad scientist's creepy lab!"

Chris nodded. "Ohhhh. Sounds awesome! You should totally write that one up. It'd be a maximum ride!"

"I can already see the movie!" added Steve.

So where'd I get the inspiration for that particular idea?

I dunno. Maybe from my dreams. Everybody dreams about flying, right? But what if that dream turned into a nightmare? What if the kids in the experiment weren't exactly willing participants?

Asking "What if?" is a great way to get a story started.

It might be a great way to get my book company started, too.

For instance, what if Billy Bonkers, the eccentric and mysterious owner of the Bonkers Big

Books factory, opened his doors to five kids who found a golden bookmark tucked inside their copies of *Charlie and the Chocolate Factory* by Roald Dahl? And what if I was one of the kids and went on the factory tour with my grandpa Moe (I don't have one, but I could make one up)? And what if all the other kids were so mean and rotten and bratty that Mr. Bonkers decided to give his factory to me because he could see that I have a good heart and would take excellent care of his dream?

Or what if I just went to work on *my* dream?

Chapter 12

Booking It

I realized that if I wanted to make my dream come true, I needed more than a folder full of ideas.

I needed to sit down with those ideas and actually turn them into stories with beginnings, middles, and ends.

Good thing Mom had a spare computer stored in the front closet because she'd just upgraded to the newer model. And since Dad had just bought a brand-new all-in-one printer that could do everything—scan, fax, print, and (I think) sew up the holes in the toes of his socks—there was an old, perfectly fine printer-that-just-prints stashed in the garage.

The garage!

Silicon Valley, where I live, is full of billion-dollar companies that started in garages. Apple Inc. Hewlett-Packard. Google.

Well, our house had a garage, too. I wasn't interested in making a billion dollars, just books.

So I set up shop and went to work. Quixote was my assistant!

Of course, I could only work in the garage when it was empty. But remember, Mom and Dad are both total workaholics! That meant our garage was car-free from five in the morning until nine at night.

Everything was fine while I was writing my first books.

That took several months of dedicated keyboard clacking. When I was finished, I could just roll my writing desk up against the rear wall. I wasn't really taking up much more space than a weed whacker.

But then I started printing out copies. Lots and lots of copies. I figured there were thousands of kids like Maddie who wanted fun books to read, and I didn't want to disappoint any of them.

So the garage became my book warehouse, too.

I guess I should've written myself a happier ending.

And then, of course, my parents came home. With their cars.

"What is all this, James?" asked Dad. (Yep. When I'm in trouble, I get the full-name treatment.)

"My dream!" I told him.

Mom eyed me suspiciously. "Your dream is to fill our entire two-car garage with boxes of paper?"

"They're books!" I told her. "*My* books."

"What?" said Dad. "What are they doing out here? All your books should be neatly organized on the bookcase in your bedroom. Alphabetical by author…"

"But these are new books," I tried to explain. "Ones I wrote."

Mom shook her head. "Why would anyone want to read a book written by a boy in middle school, Jimmy?"

"Because they're fast-paced page-turners!" I answered excitedly. "You see, in this one, there's a group of scrappy kids with wings growing out of their backs like birds. And here's an awesome sci-fi thriller about an alien hunter—"

51

Dad held up a hand to stop me. "Clean this mess up, James."

"Tonight," added Mom. "We need to park our cars. They're predicting rain in the morning."

"Put your so-called books in the recycling bins and roll them out to the curb," said Dad.

"B-b-but—"

"Now!"

"Yes, sir."

Yep. That's what I *said* I'd do.

But it wasn't what I did.

I didn't toss out anything. Nope. With a little help from my friends, I rolled it all to school!

Chapter 13

A Book's Best Friend

Where's the best place on earth to store books?

A library, of course! And Ms. Sprenkle, our school librarian, was the one grown-up who'd encouraged me to follow my dreams and do what I loved.

"I'm sure Ms. Sprenkle will let me set up shop in the media center," I told my friends as we wheeled the three recycling bins brimming with paper down the block.

"An excellent idea," said Pierce. "She is always

saying she wishes the library had more books on the shelves."

"Well," I said, "we're about to make her wish come true!"

In my mind, I could definitely imagine my new book company operating out of the school library. It had everything we needed. Computers. Printers. Even art supplies. Kids in English classes would become our authors. Kids in art classes would be our illustrators. Kids from gym class would help us push heavy stuff around.

But as much as Ms. Sprenkle wanted to support our "literary efforts," opening my book company in the school library "just wouldn't work out."

"Teachers need to use the copy machines," she explained. "And I need shelf space for all the middle school classics: *Anne of Green Gables, Because of Winn-Dixie, Bridge to Terabithia, A Connecticut Yankee in King Arthur's Court...*"

I nodded so she wouldn't go through her whole alphabetically organized list. Librarians like to organize stuff.

"Plus, I have money in my budget to buy *new* books, ones that just came out. Those will take up even more shelf space. I'm afraid there just isn't room in my library for your book company, Jimmy."

Discouraged, my friends and I hauled all the recycling bins back home. On the way, we passed a big chain bookstore sitting right next to a print-and-ship center.

This would also be an excellent place to run a book company, I thought. We could print the books at the printing place and sell them at the bookstore! We could grab any art supplies we needed from the craft shop in the same strip mall.

I told my idea to the manager of the bookstore *and* the manager of the printing place. I even told it to the lady behind the counter at the fro-yo place.

They all laughed out loud.

"Ha!" they all said. "Not gonna happen, kid. Not in a million years."

Then they all laughed out loud again.

You want to know something pretty sad?

The more grown-ups that tell a kid his or her dream can't come true, the more the kid starts to believe them.

Late that night, I rolled those three recycling bins out to the curb in front of our house, just like my father had told me to.

The next morning, the bins were empty.

My pages filled with stories were gone—gobbled up by a fleet of San Jose garbage trucks.

Or so I thought.

Yep, it's time for a plot twist! (That's writer talk for something unexpected!)

Chapter 14

G'BOSH

Turns out that this family that lives up the block and around the corner from us is super, super rich.

A few years ago, both the mom and the dad started up tech companies, which they sold to bigger tech companies for maybe a bazillion dollars. Each. So now they were double bazillionaires.

They also had a five-car garage behind their megamansion and only three cars.

I learned this all from their daughter, a very cool and confident girl named Hailey, with whitish-blond hair, whom I met on my way to school. She's my age and was biking down the block with a copy of one of my books stuffed inside her bike basket—the one about the kids with wings.

"Excuse me?" I said when I finally caught up to her. "Where'd you find that book?"

"On the street in front of a house," she said. "There were like two dozen copies of this one crammed into a garbage can. The other Dumpster had a different book. Pretty cool science-fiction adventure about aliens…"

"Actually, those were recycling bins. And that was my house."

"Oh, so you're Jimmy? The author?"

"Yeah."

"Cool. This story about the 'angel experiment' is awesome. I'm almost finished. I'm hoping to read the rest today during lunch. Or study hall. Or history. I hate history with Mr. Quackenberry. He's always telling us about the greatest failures and disasters of all time."

"I know. I have him, too."

We strolled the rest of the way to school together.

She told me how she had rescued all my books and safely stored them in her parents' garage.

"They're too good to toss out," she said.

"Thanks."

"You and your books can be big, Jimmy," she said. "But to be big, you need to think big. You know what my parents say all the time?"

"Clean up your room? Take out the trash? Don't run with scissors?"

"I mean besides all that standard stuff."

"No, what do they say all the time?"

"G'bosh!"

"Huh?"

"G-B-O-S-H. Go big or stay home!"

"Oh. Cool."

"It worked for them. They went big and ended up even bigger. Oh, and Jimmy?"

"Yeah?"

"Make me another book. Please?"

Encouraged by my new friend Hailey and her parents' awesome Go Big philosophy, I decided to give my big book company idea another, even bigger shot.

"To be big, we need to think big!" I told my friends over lunch. "We need to give this book company a big name!"

"How about Starbucks?" suggested Chris. "Everybody knows that name."

"Jimmy's not selling coffee," said Maxine.

"Okay. How about McDonald's?"

"He's not doing burgers and fries, either."

"I've got it!" I said. "Who's the biggest book company in the world?"

"I believe that would be Pearson PLC, in London," said Pierce, who sometimes knows way too many facts. "They're a publisher."

"How do you know this stuff?" asked Maxine.

"To be honest," said Pierce, "that's the one thing I don't really know."

"I'm talking about Amazon!" I said. "They're huge, which is probably why they named themselves after one of the longest rivers in the world."

"It's actually the second longest," said Pierce.

"I know! That's why we'll take the longest river and become the Nile Book Company! How's that for thinking big?"

Chris gave me a weird look. So did everybody else at the table.

"Okay. Forget the Nile. We'll go with another really long river: the Mississippi Book Company."

"I guess it's better than the Yangtze or Ob Book Company," said Pierce.

"Where are those rivers?"

"China and Russia."

I nodded. "Okay. We'll stick with the Missis-sippi. Or the Nile. I still like the Nile. How about the Hudson?"

I knew I hadn't quite found the perfect name, but thinking big inspired me to make some big changes to my plans!

Chapter 15

Streaming Books

Bouncing around all those big river names for my book company made me think about *streaming* books at my factory (pun intended). It also made me really need to pee.

Anyway, it was time for a fresh design!

Rafe came over to my house after school. Together, we sketched a new vision for our publishing company.

"At my Mississippi Book Company," I proudly announced during lunch on Friday, "nothing will slow down the rapid flow of ideas to the page, to the books, to the reader! Not even raging rapids!"

"Because," added Rafe, "the place will be like a giant water park! With water slides and waterfalls and a lazy river for the editors to drift along on, slowly making revisions!"

"Um, wouldn't water ruin the books?" asked Chris.

"Definitely," said my new friend Hailey, who'd joined us at our table. "You ever read in the bathtub? The pages get soggy. Then they're all warped and wrinkly when they dry."

"We've thought about that," said Rafe. "Right, Jimmy?"

"Yep. Which is why all the books making their way through the factory would be wrapped inside plastic bubbles. That'll also make them easier to ship, because who needs to bubble-wrap books that are already wrapped in bubbles?"

"Cool," said Chris. "Then you definitely need to put in a swimming pool, man. With a diving board. Especially for books that you want to make a big splash!"

"To help our workers keep up with the books making their way through the production pipeline,"

I said, "every kid at the book factory will be given their own personal hoverboard. Or a pair of hover-shoes."

"And a helicopter hat," added Rafe.

We showed the gang our latest sketch.

Everybody loved the new drawings.

"But how on earth are you going to build it, Jimmy?" asked Pierce.

"Not sure," I replied. "Maybe we'll use Lego."

Everybody loved that idea, too—especially since a bunch of us had been to the Legoland water park in Carlsbad, California. After the new sketches for the book company factory were passed around the cafeteria, we had a one hundred percent approval rating. All the kids in school wanted to work at the Mississippi Book Company. Or the Nile.

The grown-ups, on the other hand...Well, let's just say they thought my ideas were all wet.

But even though the grown-ups were all laughing out loud at me and my dream, it didn't get me down.

No way was I going to give up.

Because I knew a whole bunch of kids were counting on me to bring them books they actually wanted to read!

Chapter 16

Bank Shot

So I did what grown-ups do when they want to start a company and their parents aren't super rich.

I went to the bank to get a loan. That's right—it's just like in Monopoly. If you want to buy, say, Marvin Gardens, but don't have any money, you ask the banker to give you a loan. If it's my friend Chris, he usually will. Because he likes to keep the game going. He won't even make you mortgage one of your properties. He'll just slip you an orange five-hundred-dollar bill and say, "Pay me back when you can."

I figured grown-up bankers would feel the same

way. They'd loan me the money, and I'd make the books, sell the books, and pay them back their loan plus a little something extra (like, maybe, a free autographed copy of one of my books).

With my factory all sketched out and ready to be built (all we had to do was order the Lego), I figured it should be super easy. A slam dunk.

So my friends and I marched to the bank branch closest to my house, first thing on Saturday. Quixote went with us for moral support.

I even put on my bow tie. Bankers love, love, *love* bow ties.

As my pals peered through the big bank windows, I sat down with the loan officer, a nice lady named Mrs. McGillicutty. She liked my bow tie.

But not much else.

"All right, all right, all right," I said to the crowd. "You can stop. I get it. You all think a kid starting his own book company is a ridiculous, laugh-out-loud, hilarious idea."

And that's when it hit me!

What a great idea!

Forget all those rivers.

I was going to name my new company Laugh Out Loud Books!

No matter how many grown-ups loudly laughed at the idea!

Chapter 17

Mystery! Suspense! Magic!

Okay, so this is turning into a suspense novel, right?

You never know what's going to happen next because *I* never knew what was going to happen next. As I chased my dream, my whole life turned into one giant mystery.

Speaking of mysteries, that's one of my favorite genres, which is a fancy way of saying "type of book." When I first heard a teacher say *genre* I thought she was talking about a guy named John Ra. I figured he might be a flute player or something.

Anyway, mysteries are one of my favorite kinds of story. I love Carl Hiaasen's *Flush* and *Hoot*. I couldn't put down *The London Eye Mystery* by Siobhan Dowd. And I love, love, *love* the whole Young Sherlock Holmes series by Andrew Lane, especially *Death Cloud*.

When I started my own book company, I knew we'd definitely be doing a whole bunch of mysteries and thrillers.

Okay, enough with the suspense. I can't keep you dangling off a cliff forever. The rope might snap.

So here's what happened next.

After my terrible, horrible, no-good, very bad day at the bank, I woke up the next morning and there was a snowy-white owl sitting in my bedroom. He was perched on the back of my homework chair. There was a letter clutched in his beak.

It was junk mail from a local carpet cleaning company.

But—there was another rolled-up scroll of parchment tied to the owl's left talon! I put on my favorite Harry Potter robe and scarf, unscrolled the missive, and read it.

Shazam!

All of a sudden, I had magical powers. I didn't even have to go to a wizard school called Hogwarts or Pigpimples. I was like a modern-day Harry Potter, without the scar or glasses.

Yep, I could do incredible magic.

For instance, I could make our school bus fly.

I put our super-serious history teacher Mr. Quackenberry under a jokelorum spell so everything he said was hysterical.

And, in my biggest magical feat of them all, I made the pizza bread in the cafeteria actually taste like something besides cardboard smeared with ketchup.

"Whoa," said my buddy Chris, enjoying his lunch. "You really are a wizard."

"Shazambalamba bop!" I said, waving my arms around and using my number two soft lead pencil as a magic wand.

A squadron of owls flew into the cafeteria and dropped everybody a box of glazed doughnuts. *Hot* glazed doughnuts.

It was time to go home and put on my magic act for the toughest crowd in the world: my parents!

Chapter 18

Home Field Advantage

Later that night, Mom and Dad were in the dining room, once again hunkered over stacks of paper they'd brought home from work.

As usual, they didn't even know I was there. It was like I was wearing an invisibility cloak, which maybe I was, seeing as how I'd recently become a certified Harry Potter–style magician.

"Guess what, you guys?" I announced. "I'm officially a wizard!"

"That's nice, dear," said Mom without looking up from a manila folder jammed with legal briefs.

"It's true. I have magical powers!"

"Uhm-hmm," mumbled Dad. "Have you been reading *The Hobbit* again?"

"Yes. But that's not what this is all about. You see, a wise messenger owl flew into my bedroom. Tied to his talon with a leather thong was a missive, which is really just a word that means 'note,' but *missive* sounds much more magical, don't you think?"

"Uhm-hmm," said Mom.

"That's nice," said Dad.

Yep, neither one of them was paying any attention. I could've said an elephant flew into my bedroom and they still wouldn't've looked up from their papers.

It was time for a demonstration. I held up my number two soft lead pencil and flicked my wrist.

"What the—?" said Dad. "All these tax returns just magically filled themselves in."

"And," I pronounced, with another wave of my wand, "all of your clients will be receiving huge refunds!"

"Amazing," said Dad.

I had his full, undivided attention.

Mom's, too!

"Jimmy, can you magically help me file this motion on behalf of my client?"

I whipped up a quick legalbeaglemus spell.

"Done and done! Your client will be awarded three times the money they were suing for!"

"Wow," said Mom and Dad.

"Work's finished!" I said. "It's time for family game night!"

And so we all played Monopoly. With floating motels and talking tokens!

I realized something amazing: I could use my newfound magical powers to create my book company!

I waved my number two soft lead pencil over a ream of paper.

Shazamalamadingdong!

I conjured up two complete books! I could've waved my wand seven more times and written seven more sequels, but I figured that would've just been showing off.

Chapter 19

Sticky Notes

Okay, okay, okay.

Nothing from those last two chapters actually happened. At least not because I was a wizard with a magic pencil wand.

But while I was telling the story, it all seemed so real. Even the white owl, which was really this pigeon with white feathers that likes to perch on the windowsill outside my bedroom so it can poop on Mom's rosebushes below.

Gosh, I love stories.

Especially stories about magic. And pigeons.

But magic isn't how I started my book company.

Nope. That took lots and lots of hard work. And sticky notes. Lots and lots of those, too.

It was a Saturday. Mom and Dad went to their offices because they both had to work that weekend.

I read a book after breakfast (*The Crossover* by Kwame Alexander—which, by the way, actually makes poetry cool), then went to work.

I started jotting down ideas on sticky notes. Before long, my ideas were like potato chips, peanuts, or pimples. I couldn't have just one. I had a billion of them.

Before long, the stickies were climbing the walls of my room. So were a bunch of photographs and sketches. And three-by-five index cards. And newspaper clippings. I connected ideas that went together with yarn and string.

When there was no more wall space, I started posting stuff on the window shades. And the desk lamp. And my computer screen. When I ran out of vertical spaces, I grabbed a ladder and started posting notes and clippings and photographs on the ceiling.

My mind was racing, and I'd only had one Coca-Cola for breakfast. I was like Katniss Everdeen. I was a boy on fire!

"What's all this?" Mom asked when she and Dad came home that night.

"Ideas!" I told her. "Inspiration!"

"Well, it's your room, Jimmy. You can decorate it any way you want…"

"Personally, I would've gone with a sports motif," said Dad. "You know—team jerseys. Bobble-head dolls. A spongy 'we're number one' foam finger. But like your mother said, it's your bed-room, Jimmy. If you want to go with a whole Post-it notes and detective's wall theme, that's fine by us."

When they left, Quixote came over and nuzzled up against my leg.

I could tell—my faithful canine companion still believed in me and my dream.

So did Yertle, my turtle.

The big question, the giant, flying elephant in the room, was...

Did I still believe in myself?

I wasn't so sure. Especially when I started

imagining all those notes and pictures on the wall laughing at me.

Yep. They were laughing out loud!

Chapter 20

Speaking Up for Myself

Luckily, my friends at school still loved my idea.

"We don't need any more broccoli books," said Chris Grabbetts. "You know—ones that are supposed to be good for you. We need books kids actually want to read!"

"All kinds of kids," added Kenny Wilson. "Even kids with a secret identity who might actually be superheroes but nobody knows that about them because everybody thinks they're just, you know, the captain of the chess team and a grandma's boy because nobody's ever seen them in their totally fly superhero costume."

"Kenny, aren't you captain of the chess team?" Chris asked.

"Who, me? What! N-no..." Kenny stammered.

I just sort of nodded, and filed an idea away in my brain for another book: a mild-mannered schoolkid who can turn into a superhero, just like Clark Kent turns into Superman.

"Don't let anyone discourage you, Jimmy," said Maxine.

"Not even the inanimate objects on your walls," added Rafe. "Were they really laughing at you, man?"

"Yep," I said, tapping my temple. "In my imagination."

"Whoa. That's where they're loudest."

The bell rang and we all headed off to class.

First period on Monday, I had English with Mrs. Delvecchio. English used to be my favorite subject until I got into Mrs. Delvecchio's class. I still liked it because I got to spend a lot of time reading stories by amazing authors. Mark Twain. Edgar Allan Poe.

Ray Bradbury. But, well, it just wasn't as much fun because Mrs. Delvecchio didn't think learning should be fun. It was our job.

"All right, class, kindly put your books away," said Mrs. Delvecchio, who droned in a monotone. "I'm waiting. Still waiting. Good. Today, we are going to continue our exploration of English and the power of words with another five-minute extemporaneous speech."

Mrs. Delvecchio was big on what she called *forensics*. It wasn't the kind of cool forensics they use on all those *CSI* shows. This forensics was "the practice and study of formal debate." We all had to be prepared, at all times, to give a persuasive speech off the top of our heads.

"James?" said Mrs. Delvecchio, checking the list of names in her grade book.

Yep. She never called me Jimmy. She was way too serious for that.

"Today is your lucky day. Of course I say that *ironically* and somewhat *sardonically*, two words that are on your vocabulary list this week."

"Yes, ma'am." I stood up.

"You can't use any notes."

"Notes?" I said with a confident laugh. "I don't need any notes."

"Good. Because, as I stated previously, you cannot use them."

"Yes, ma'am. Right. Got it."

For the record, Mrs. Delvecchio doesn't really have what you might call a sense of humor.

"You have five minutes, James. Go!"

I was off like a rocket!

"Ladies and gentlemen, today I'd like to talk to you about my dream. Sometime, very soon, I am going to start a book company for kids that's run by kids who know exactly what other kids want to read!"

"Woo-hoo!" shouted Chris. "Tell 'em, brother!"

"We're going to make reading fun for kids because the more something is fun, the more it gets done!"

"That's right!" cried Kenny.

"It will be the most incredible book company in the entire world. Our books will take kids on exciting adventures! We'll open their eyes to whole new worlds and new ways of looking at things! My Laugh Out Loud Book Company will have a river flowing through it—a river filled with floating books. We'll have a Ferris wheel instead of a freight elevator, too! Why? Because Ferris wheels are more fun! And all the employees will ride hoverboards. Real hoverboards. The kind without any wheels! They'll just float above the floor, the way a good book makes us float above a dull and ordinary world!"

Yep, I gave a very rousing five-minute speech.

All the kids in the class were going wild. They were cheering for me and my dream! They knew my cause was just and right and good!

When I finished at four minutes and fifty-nine seconds, the classroom erupted in applause.

I was a hit!

Until I wasn't.

Chapter 21

Bursting
My Bubble

My hit missed. Big-time.

Mrs. Delvecchio totally burst my bubble.

"James," said Mrs. Delvecchio, "in my classroom, an extemporaneous talk must be based on facts. Research. It can't be fiction."

My buddy Chris raised his hand.

"Yes, Mr. Grabbetts?"

"Um, how can Jimmy do research if he has to, you know, do the talk without any prep?"

"I expect my students to come to class with solid facts stored inside their brains. Not farfetched, pie-in-the-sky, fantastical castles in the air. I want real-world information. Not make-believe nonsense."

"But Mrs. Delvecchio," I said, "this isn't make-believe. I'm already working on it. I'm really going to start a book company run by kids!"

"Nonsense. Children your age don't know what children should be reading."

"We don't?"

"Of course not."

Totally defeated, I slumped down in my chair.

"I liked your speech," whispered Maxine, seated behind me.

"I thought it was awesome," whispered Chris.

"You are failing the mission!" barked a tinny voice outside the window.

94

The aliens were back. They'd landed in the school parking lot, just outside Mrs. Delvecchio's classroom. The guy with the bulging brain bubble and ginormous eyes was glaring at me. Marvin the Martian had his ray gun aimed at me again, too.

"Ooh, you are making me very, very mad!" said Marvin.

"I can't believe this," I mumbled.

"That is why you fail," said Yoda. "Trust your imagination you must."

"I'm working on it," I told Yoda. "You should see all the sticky notes on my bedroom walls and ceiling. Patience you must have."

"My line that is," he answered back.

"James?" It was Mrs. Delvecchio. "Why are you staring out that window while I am attempting to reprimand you for your shoddy oratorical performance?"

"Um, I was just sort of daydreaming..."

"And that's precisely your problem. During the day, you're supposed to work, not dream. School is your job!"

"Yes, ma'am."

"You need to grow up, James. You also need to prepare another speech. A speech filled with facts, not flights of fancy."

"B-b-but..."

"And you never know when I might call on you. Tomorrow? Next week? Next month? I can only offer you two words of advice: Be prepared! Because if you're not, if your next speech is as awful as your first, you will receive an F in English this semester."

"Whoa," said Chris. "That's kind of harsh."

"Would you like to give your speech *today*, Mr. Grabbetts?"

"Um, no. Not really."

"Then keep quiet. The choice is yours, James. A new, fact-filled speech or an F. And let me remind you: Nobody wants to read a book by an author who received an F in English. That would be like going to a brain surgeon who flunked biology!"

Chapter 22

Be Like Bud

After school, I was kind of, sort of, heartbroken and crushed.

Oh, who am I kidding?

I was *totally* heartbroken and crushed. Despondent, dejected, and downcast, too (because every good writer needs to keep a thesaurus handy at all times).

An F in English, my favorite subject?

An F in English?

That was just wrong. Mrs. Delvecchio was just

wrong. Heck, the whole world was feeling wrong and completely out of whack.

AN F IN ENGLISH?!?!?!?

So, after screaming at the sky for a while, I walked to the nearest branch of the San Jose Public Library to think things through.

I started in the fiction section, of course, because I believe you can find the best answers to real-life problems in imaginary worlds.

I picked up a copy of one of my all-time favorites, *Bud, Not Buddy* by Christopher Paul Curtis. It's my go-to novel when I need a quick refresher on perseverance and not giving up. Bad news (and there's a ton of it in the book) never seems to get Bud, the main character, down for long.

For instance, when he learns that the woman he's looking for in Flint, Michigan, has moved to Chicago, he doesn't quit. "How long would it take someone to walk that far?" he asks. "Fifty-four hours!" he's told.

That doesn't stop Bud. He perseveres.

I needed to be more like Bud.

And I wouldn't need to walk all the way to Chicago to do it—just over to the shelves where the library kept all its business books. If Mrs. Delvecchio wanted a speech filled with facts, I'd give her some. I'd back up my dream with rock-solid research.

Of course, I was the only kid perusing the business section of the library. The only one not wearing a business suit, too.

I grabbed a bunch of titles.

One was called *The Disney Way: Harnessing the Management Secrets of Disney in Your Company*. That sounded awesome. Hey, I love Disneyland.

I pulled another title off the shelf: *The Lean Startup: How Today's Entrepreneurs Use Continuous Innovation to Create Radically Successful Businesses*.

I was so glad my dream wasn't to start a business-book company. The titles are way too long.

I creaked open the Disney business book.

One of the grown-ups shushed me. His shush was way louder than my creak.

"Did you know," whispered another grown-up at the reading table, "that eighty percent of all new businesses fail?"

The other grown-up shushed her, too.

That's when a librarian came over.

"Excuse me, young man," she said. "Juvenile books are located downstairs in the children's department. These business books are intended for adults with serious business ideas."

"But I need to do some research on how to start up my company."

A giggle bubbled up inside her. "You're kidding."

The other two grown-ups covered their mouths and tried not to laugh.

"I'm super serious, you guys," I told them. "I'm going to start a book company run by kids."

The librarian laughed out loud at me. So did the two grown-ups in suits. Before long, the three of them were guffawing louder than the laugh track on an old-fashioned sitcom.

Guess they all forgot we were in a library.

Chapter 23

Street Corner Inspiration

I was still feeling pretty low when I left the library.

I'd only had a chance to jot down a few facts for my speech before all the grown-ups laughing out loud at me made it impossible to focus. My notes went something like this: "Write a business plan. Ha, ha, ha. Do market analysis. Ha, ha, ha."

I still needed more information for my extemporaneous talk, which Mrs. Delvecchio could spring on me as early as the next day!

I decided to head to the nearest grocery store to do that market analysis thing.

But on my way, I saw this kid in a wheelchair.

He was crossing the street and approaching a curb that was maybe six inches tall. Right before he hit the curb, he stopped. I guessed he'd just realized that the city hadn't made that particular section of sidewalk "wheelchair accessible" yet. There was no built-in ramp or slope. Just that hard ledge.

The kid in the chair grinned and rolled backward a few feet. Smiling wider, he pumped his wheels hard and raced toward the curb to build up momentum. Right before he hit the concrete slab, he leaned back to pop a wheelie!

The instant his front wheels cleared the curb, he leaned forward and brought his rear wheels up and over the cement cliff, too.

It was very inspirational.

I couldn't help rushing over to tell him how cool he looked.

"Thanks," he said. "I just can't stand these sidewalks. Then again, I just can't stand."

I laughed. Then I thought maybe I shouldn't've laughed. So I stopped. But then he laughed. So I laughed. It was a regular laugh fest.

In fact, the kid in the chair, who could've been grim and sour, was extremely funny.

"Hey," he said, "have you ever seen an older lady in a wheelchair with a blanket draped over her legs?"

"Sure."

"Don't let her fool you, my friend. She's really a retired mermaid! Well, I've got to go. Fortunately, there's a handicapped stall in the coffee shop's bathroom.

"That reminds me—the other day, I went to my doctor. I told him every time I drank coffee I got a stabbing pain in my right eye. He said I should take the spoon out of the cup."

The kid was doing more than making me crack

up. He was giving me a cool idea. It wasn't exactly about my book company. But then again, maybe it was.

I thought about the way he'd attacked that curb when he could've just given up. How he could've wallowed in the gutter and waited until someone came along to give him a helpful tilt and push.

I thought about the way he laughed and cracked jokes when he could've been sad and glum.

How he just wouldn't give up, no matter what!

Yep. He gave me an idea for a story.

A story about a funny, scrappy kid who won't give up, no matter what.

For instance, what if that kid in the wheelchair wanted to become a stand-up comic even though he couldn't actually stand up?

What if he was a kid with big dreams and all sorts of obstacles to overcome, sort of like me?

I was definitely going to turn that story into a book.

And I knew exactly what I'd call it: *He Funny*.

Chapter 24

Fun Raising

First period the next day, Mrs. Delvecchio called on somebody else to give an extemporaneous speech in English class.

It was totally boring but Mrs. Delvecchio gave the guy an "A-plus, plus, plus!" because it was filled with facts. Yep. It was a real snoozer. There were a lot of heads on desks when he finished. Some open-mouth drooling, too.

"Don't worry, Jimmy," said Rafe after class. "You still have time to become that boring. It's an acquired skill."

"I read a bunch of business books yesterday," I admitted. "I'm on my way."

"Excellent."

"But I don't want to be boring," I said. "I want to tell stories that grab kids' attention. Not ones that put 'em to sleep."

"But," said Rafe, "if you have a bunch of random factoids in your speech, ye shall escape the dragon lady's lair unscorched! Ye shall dodge her fiery wrath and live to spend another day in the dark and dreary dungeon known as middle school!"

Rafe showed me a drawing he'd doodled in his notebook. It was awesome!

"So," asked Chris as we all ambled down the hall, "how much money did those business books say you needed to get your book company rolling?"

"A ton," I said. "Maybe more. To be honest, I sort of skimmed the blah-blah sections with all the numbers. Plus, the books all wanted me to write a business plan when what I really want to write are stories."

"So we'll help you," said Maxine. "How much coinage do you think you need, right away?"

"It depends," I said, turning to Rafe. "How much would it cost to get you to doodle a bunch more illustrations like that one?"

"Huh?"

"I want to do an illustrated book. All about a kid in middle school. He's a round peg in a square hole. He wants to be creative, to think outside the box, but his teachers and the principal just want him to follow the rules and be boring. One of his teachers is a real dragon lady..."

Yes, I was going to write the book I'd imagined back when I thought I had wizarding abilities.

(Which maybe I sort of did, since I was able to create stories out of thin air.)

"I just need to buy some fresh Sharpies and a sketchpad," said Rafe with a shrug.

"And I'll need enough cash to run off copies of our book," I said.

"We'll be your Kickstarter campaign!" said Chris.

"Totally," added Maxine. "We can raise all the money you need to publish your first book."

"How?" I asked.

"Car wash!" everybody answered at once.

That weekend, all my friends pitched in. Hailey, Maxine, Kenny, Chris, Steve, Maddie's little brother. Everybody.

We held a car wash. We sold used books. We had a bake sale.

We had a blast!

By the end of Saturday, we'd raised sixty-three dollars.

It wasn't much.

But it was enough!

Chapter 25

Buried Treasure

On Sunday, the Laugh Out Loud Book Company's "Kickstarter" fund took in another seventy-three cents.

And I picked up another idea for a book!

This one came from two kids who live down the block from me. They're twins, named Bob and Abby Kipplemeyer.

For whatever reason, they're always grabbing shovels out of their mom's garden shed and digging stuff up in their backyard.

"Check it out, Jimmy," said Bob. He was holding a rusty Band-Aid box caked with mud and a clump of grass.

"We found it near the oak tree," said his sister, Abby.

"The exact same spot where we found that ancient plastic dinosaur," said Bob.

"No," said Abby. "We found the dinosaur buried in the sandbox."

"No," said Bob. "It was under the oak tree."

"Sandbox."

"Oak tree!"

"SANDBOX!"

"OAK! TREE!"

"Was not."

"Was too."

"Not."

"Too."

"Not!"

"Too!"

"Three!"

"What?"

"I dunno. You said two again so I said three."

"Oh. Cool. I was kind of thinking the same thing."

"I know. It's a twin thing."

And then, smiling (even though they'd just been arguing with each other), they popped open the hinged lid on their tiny tin treasure chest.

"There's seventy-three pennies inside!" said Bob.

"And worms," added Abby.

Seeing the worms squiggling and slithering around the copper coins reminded me of another all-time favorite book: *How to Eat Fried Worms* by Thomas Rockwell (but I really wasn't in the mood for a wiggly squiggly ketchup/mustard/relish-dipped dessert).

"We want to give you this money we found for your book company," said Abby. "But not the worms. We're setting the worms free."

"Releasing them into the wild," added Bob. "Then we'll go back to digging."

"We're hoping there might be more money buried near the tree."

"Maybe even a sack of nickels!"

"Happy treasure hunting," I told them as they raced back home to dig more holes in their backyard.

And just like that—BA–LING!—I had another idea for another book!

Chapter 26

My First Real Book!

I tucked that treasure hunters brainstorm away in my thick (and growing thicker all the time) idea folder.

I had to focus on writing my story about the artistic kid having the worst years of his life in middle school.

I fired up my computer and, once again, set up shop in the garage. Since I was just writing, not printing, I didn't take up too much space. Mom and Dad didn't even notice I was there.

I decided to name my main character, who liked to doodle cool drawings, after my buddy Rafe because Rafe was the coolest doodler I knew.

Whenever I finished a chapter, I'd email the text

to Rafe, who'd come up with a couple of sketches to illustrate each chapter. Sometimes he went wild and did an illustration that took up two whole pages—in the book biz we call that a spread.

For a week, I typed and Rafe drew.

Then I typed some more.

And Rafe drew some more.

We kept at it, only taking breaks to go to school (and to the bathroom) for maybe two months. I wasn't getting much sleep or eating very well, but I was having so much fun! Rafe, too. Fortunately, Mrs. Delvecchio didn't call on me to give my extemporaneous speech while Rafe and I were creating our book. If she had, I might've called her a dragon lady.

Finally, we put everything together and took it to the copy shop at the strip mall.

"You want it bound?" asked the clerk.

"Yes," I told him.

"And you want this four-color illustration for a cover?"

"Yes," said Rafe. "And can you print the cover on thicker paper?"

"That'll make it feel more like a book," I added.

"No problemo," said the clerk. "So, how many copies do you dudes want?"

I checked the Laugh Out Loud Book Company's bank account, which was all the cash and coins tucked into my pants pockets. After paying for Rafe's art supplies plus a couple of energy drinks to keep us both going, we had maybe fifty bucks left. Actually, fifty dollars and seventy-three cents, thanks to the Kipplemeyer twins.

"Um, how many copies can we get for fifty dollars and, uh, seventy-three cents?"

"Three hundred pages bound with a card-stock cover?" said the clerk, tapping numbers into a whirring calculator.

He tore off the tape.

Read our answer.

"One."

"Okay," I said. "One copy."

"It's our first book," said Rafe.

The clerk flipped through a few pages. Checked out some of the illustrations. Laughed. Read some more pages. Laughed some more.

I realized there might be a problem writing books that readers just didn't want to put down. It might be difficult to get people who were supposed to be *printing* the books to do anything but read 'em.

Finally, the clerk shuffled all the loose paper together to make a tight stack.

"Your first book, huh?" he said.

"Yep," I replied.

"Well, I can guarantee you one thing, little dudes: It won't be your last! You've got mad skills!"

Chapter 27

Now What?

We grabbed our bound book when it was hot off the presses. Literally. The thing was still toasty warm from the copy machine.

"Now what do we do?" asked Rafe.

"Well," I said, remembering some of the most basic junk from those business books, "if we really want to be a book company we should probably sell it to somebody—for more than it cost us to make! That way we could make a profit, which, uh, is the 'excess of income over expenditure.'"

"Huh?"

"Don't worry. It'll be in my speech."

"Good. I'll sleep through that part."

"Making a profit is what makes capitalism work."

"Seriously?" said Rafe. "Isn't that, you know, cheating? Jacking up the price like that? Making more money than we spent?"

"Nope. Because if we make a profit we can make more books. In fact, I think we should sell this copy for double what it cost us to print it: one hundred dollars!"

"Um, shouldn't we just say ninety-nine ninety-nine? Every price they advertise on TV always ends with a ninety-nine. Three ninety-nine. Nine ninety-nine. Fourteen thousand nine hundred and ninety-nine..."

"Good idea."

We knocked knuckles on it.

"Now," I said, "we just need to find somebody who has ninety-nine dollars and ninety-nine cents."

"Whoa," said Rafe. "That's nearly one hundred bucks. Who do we know with that kind of cash?"

He was right. None of our friends (except maybe Hailey) got a very large allowance. And even if they did, some of their weekly money had to go to purchasing everyday essentials. You know—stuff like bubble gum, video games, and lip gloss.

And then it hit me.

"Who do we know who actually has a budget for buying books?"

"Um, the rotund dude with the man-bun who runs the Comic Book Shoppe?"

"We'll hit him up later," I said. "When we have more copies that he can sell to his customers."

"Cool. So who's our first customer?"

"Ms. Sprenkle! The librarian at school! Remember, she told us she had to keep room on her shelves for all the new books she was going to buy? Well, this is the newest book in town!"

The next morning, Rafe and I raced to the school library the second we got off the bus.

"Congratulations," said Ms. Sprenkle when we showed her our book. "You are a published author, Jimmy. And you, Rafe, are a published illustrator."

"And we're both ready for our first book sale!" said Rafe.

"What's the cover price?" she asked.

"Ninety-nine ninety-nine," I told her.

She arched an eyebrow.

"But," I said, "there's a school library discount. Schools only have to pay ninety dollars. That's nearly ten percent off!"

"That's very expensive for one book."

"It's a limited edition!" I said. "A first and only printing!"

She smiled. "Can I read it first?"

"Sure."

"Good. Come back after lunch. If I like it, we have a deal. I think it's very important that the library encourage young authors just getting started."

As you might've guessed, it felt like the

loooooongest lunch in history. Longer than one of those Henry the Eighth banquets where everybody gobbled down turkey drumsticks with their bare hands.

At one o'clock, Rafe and I raced back into the library.

Ms. Sprenkle was standing there waiting for us with a big smile on her face.

She also had four twenties and a ten in her hand!

Chapter 28

I ♥ Librarians!

"I'd give your book a gold star, boys," said Ms. Sprenkle. "I believe you have artfully woven a deep and thought-provoking tale of childhood coping mechanisms and everyday school and family realities."

Oh-kay. We just thought we made up a funny story about a kid breaking all the dumb rules at his stuck-in-the-mud middle school.

But whatever.

Our first review was a starred review, because

the librarian prominently displayed our book on the top shelf of a corner bookcase with a "Ms. Sprenkle's Choice" star made out of cardboard and gold foil wrapping paper.

"Whoa," said Rafe. "Only really good books get the gold star!"

"It's like we're a staff pick at a bookstore," I said to Ms. Sprenkle. "Except, you know, you don't sell books. You just lend them out."

"Correct," said Ms. Sprenkle. "And I have already entered your illustrated novel into the computer card catalog. Students can start checking it out immediately."

"I want it!" said Rafe.

"Um, shouldn't we let somebody who hasn't already read it check it out first?" I suggested.

"Oh. Good point."

"So," asked Ms. Sprenkle, "what are you guys going to do with the ninety dollars? Buy a video game? Download a few apps?"

"No, ma'am. If the guy at the copy shop will give us a bulk discount, we're going to print two more copies of our book!"

Luckily, the dude at the copy store really, really, *really* liked our story.

"It's like you wrote *my* story, man!" he told us when we returned to his store. "I chewed gum in class. I dressed funky. I even thought about pulling the fire alarm once. I was a bad boy with a heart of gold, just like Rafe."

"Thanks," said the real Rafe. "I guess."

Anyway, the copy guy liked *Middle School* so

much, he did give us a discount: two copies for ninety dollars!

"Write on, little dude!" he said, giving me a raised-fist salute when the job was all done. "Write on!"

We took the two books to school with us.

There was an awesome English teacher (not Mrs. Delvecchio) who'd taught me the year before. Her name was Tara Muenk. She had the best, coolest classroom library of anyone at the middle school.

"I always knew you'd become a writer, Jimmy," she said, hugging my book the way I'd hugged it the day before. "Chris Grabbetts, too."

"Because he has good penmanship?"

Ms. Muenk grinned. "Is that what he told you?"

"Yeah. That he, you know, liked the 'writing' part. Doing calligraphy and junk."

Ms. Muenk laughed. "That's because Chris Grabbetts is always cracking jokes and trying to be the class clown. But he has real talent. Trust me. Hey, maybe you two should work together. Collaborate."

I nodded. It was a good idea. If I had a couple of authors to write with, I could make more books with all the ideas stuffed in my head and my file folder. When kids said, "Give me another book, Jimmy," they wouldn't have to wait so long if I had other writers working with me.

Long story short, Ms. Muenk bought both copies from the second printing of my first book.

We had one hundred and eighty dollars in the bank, which was still the pocket of my jeans.

"Now we can print four more books!" said Rafe.

"Or," I suggested, "we could celebrate the official birth of my book company with a pizza party extravaganza!"

"An excellent idea," said Rafe. "Because we've been working so hard, I'm starving!"

"Yeah," I said. "Me too."

And so my new book company planned its first-ever office party!

Chapter 29

PAR-TAY!

That night, we had the best pizza party one hundred and eighty dollars can buy!

I'm talking Papa John's *and* Pizza Hut. They were both having specials. So we ordered a few pepperoni pies plus garlic knots, cheesy bread, and jalapeño poppers. Yep, there was a lot of extra gas in our garage. We also scored one of those ginormous chocolate chip cookies the size of a manhole cover.

After everybody had chowed down and danced the Dab, I decided it was time for me to make a speech. I bopped the side of a two-liter bottle of soda to get everybody's attention. Chris shut off the dance music.

"You guys?" I said. "I just wanted to say that I'll never forget this day. You guys are my inspiration. My muses. You were also my first investors!"

"Woo-hoo!" everybody shouted.

"It was your car washing skills that gave us enough money to make my dream a reality. Sure, we've only printed three copies of our first book, but like they say, every journey starts with a small acorn. No, wait a second. Strike that. They say mighty oak trees take small steps. No, no. That's not it, either."

Everybody started laughing, which is exactly what I wanted them to do. Hey, if you're running a company called Laugh Out Loud Books, there better be some laugh-out-loud moments in the workday, not to mention the par-tay.

"Actually, what they say is 'Hey, Jimmy—please give me another book.'"

Everybody cheered when I said that. (Note to self: Have that slogan printed on T-shirts.)

Just then, the garage door started rising, slowly grinding its way up.

Mom and Dad were home from work.

"What's going on?" asked Mom from behind the wheel.

"Why's everybody having fun?" asked Dad.

"Jimmy sold his first books!" shouted Chris.

"So we're having a party to celebrate," said Maxine.

"We need to park our vehicles," said Mom.

"Let's clean up this mess, kids," said Dad.

Mess? Wow. Talk about a party pooper.

All my friends were bummed, but they chipped in and helped out. We cleaned up all the pizza crusts and stacked the cardboard cartons in the recycling bin.

Have I told you how amazingly awesome my friends are?

That's another reason I wanted to open up a full-scale book-making factory ASAP. So we could all work together and hang out together every day. It'd be fun, like at school. There just wouldn't be so much homework.

Chris Grabbetts was the last to leave. He helped me roll the trash and recycling bins down to the curb. It was late but the moon was shining bright.

"Great party," said Chris.

"You know what?" I said to him. "When I open my company, every day will feel like a party!"

"Hey, Jimmy!"

It was Sammy, my next-door neighbor.

"Hey, Sammy. What's up?"

"Maddie." He gestured over his shoulder. My other next-door neighbor was up on the second floor, waving at me from her glowing bedroom window. "She heard about the new book you wrote. The one about middle school with all the funny drawings. She wants a copy."

"Yeah," said Chris. "So do I."

And that's when I realized what a huge mistake the whole pizza party thing was.

My Laugh Out Loud bank vault was completely empty. We had no more cash on hand.

And without cash, we couldn't run off more copies of my first book—no matter how much the dude at the copy shop loved it.

Chapter 30

Banking on a New Bank

Monday, right after school, I put on my bow tie again and went to a new bank.

This one was an "investment bank" in San Jose called Adventurous Venture Capital, Inc. According to their website, they were famous for providing "seed money" to Silicon Valley start-ups. Why software developers needed seeds, I had no idea. Maybe they liked to make popcorn while they wrote code.

Anyway, I biked over to Adventurous Venture Capital's offices. Everything inside was very sleek and modern. Their lobby reminded me of a piece of furniture from that IKEA store.

"Please take a seat," said the receptionist. "One of our investment specialists will be with you shortly."

I took a seat.

But it turns out *shortly* meant "in maybe an hour, maybe two."

I spent the time flipping through magazines. A lot of them were filled with success stories about tech companies worth billions that had started as somebody's dream. They were my kind of success stories! I figured if they could do it, so could I— with just a little help.

Finally, three bankers came marching into the lobby.

"You wished to see us?" said number one.

"Yes, ma'am."

"This way," said number two.

"Follow us to the conference room," said number three.

Then, like synchronized swimmers, they all pivoted on their heels and led the way to another glass-walled aquarium room.

"Tell us your idea," said number one when they were all seated across a table from me.

"Make your pitch," said number two.

"But please be efficient," said number three, checking something on his wristwatch. "Apparently, my son has a softball game this evening."

"You got it!" I said, standing up. "Here we go."

I told them we had "proof of concept," because that was one of the phrases I found in all those *How to Start Your Own Business* books.

"We ran off three copies of our first title and— BOOM! Everybody wants to buy it. We're going viral. Not that we're making people sick, but word of mouth is spreading like crazy!"

I told them about all my ideas for books. How I wanted to create books that made reading fun.

I pitched with gusto and passion and maybe too many arm gestures (I knocked a water bottle off the table).

But all I got in return were long faces and robotic responses.

"Interesting."

"What's your cost of goods?"

"Who is your target market?"

"Enter your zip code."

"Press the pound key."

"If you'd like to talk to a real human being, go outside and find one."

I guess I should've been upset. Instead, I started grinning. These robotic bankers were giving me another idea for a book!

Chapter 31

Robo-Bankers

"Robots!" I blurted. "You three remind me of robots, which is totally awesome!"

"Come again?" said the first banker.

"You guys just gave me another idea for a book kids will love."

"Please clarify," said the frowning banker seated directly across from me.

"Kids love robots! They make 'em. They remote-control 'em. They ask for 'em on their birthdays. Well, what if I did another illustrated book about a world where all the characters—the teachers, the

principals, the lunch ladies, even the bankers—
were robots? I could write it with Chris Grabbetts.
We'd find a fantastic illustrator to do the drawings.
Maybe even somebody from Canada!"

The venture capitalists frowned in unison. It
was like they were all sharing the same operating
system!

"No, wait," I said as a new idea flashed across
my mind. "This is even better. Forget Robo-World.
My next book will be about a kid who lives in a
house full of robots. His mother is some kind of
genius scientist slash professor. His sister is very sick
and stuck in her room all day so the mom makes

robots to help her out. One has whirling brushes and dust mops to sanitize her room. Another is a robo-dog to keep her company! And there's this really smart robot named Einstein or Egghead that helps her learn stuff, since she's too sick to go to a real school…"

"You wish us to invest in a robotic dog named Eggstein who does light housecleaning chores?" asked one of the confused bankers.

"No. I want you to help me open the Laugh Out Loud Book Company so I can publish this really cool idea. I already have a title for it: *Rooms Full of Robots*!"

The three bankers swiveled their heads and nodded at each other. I could almost hear the whirr and click of their servos and gears.

"We regret to inform you," said the lady banker, "that your request for financial support has been denied."

"No. This is my dream. You can't deny a dream!"

"Yes," said number one. "It is what we do."

"On a regular basis," added number two.

"It makes us feel powerful and important," said three.

I tried to protest. "But—"

"Denied."

"Just hear me out—"

"Negative. You have been denied."

"Okay. Maybe I shouldn't've called you guys robots…"

"Denied, denied, denied!"

The woman stood up. "This customer service interface will terminate in ten seconds."

"B-b-but—"

"Five."

I leapt out of my chair and ran for the door.

I wanted to be out of the building when the lids blew off their robotic heads.

Chapter 32

The Friendly Neighborhood Billionaire

When I hit the sidewalk, I was ready to give up.

To throw in the towel. To call it quits. *No way is anybody going to help me make my dream come true,* I thought. Grown-ups weren't going to lend me money to start the Laugh Out Loud Book Company. They'd just keep laughing out loud at me.

"Excuse me, young man."

I nearly stopped breathing. Steve Grates, the world-famous multimultibillionaire tech tycoon— the guy who created that app where a car comes to pick you up before you even tell it to—had just stepped out of the investment bank, and he was talking to *me*. At least I thought he was. To make sure, I looked around—just to be certain there weren't any other "young men" hanging around on the sidewalk.

Mr. Grates laughed. "Yes, I'm talking to you. What's your name?"

"Jimmy."

"Hi, Jimmy. I'm Steve."

He shot out his hand.

"Uh, hiya, Steve." I shook it.

Grates was wearing the same purple turtleneck sweater he always wore. I figured he had to have like six dozen in his closet. Otherwise, I would've smelled some serious BO.

"You know," said the multimultibillionaire, "I remember trying to start up my first company. I had this brilliant idea: a computer that doubled as a microwave oven. I used the CD/DVD drive as a food tray. All you had to do was flatten your Hot Pocket, pizza slice, or Pop-Tart, load it in, and thirty seconds later—DING! You'd be enjoying a piping-hot meal without ever having to leave your keyboard. It was brilliant!"

Dinner: Solved!

"People called me a dreamer," he said. "They said I was too young to start a company. They said my pizza-making idea would never work. And they were right. It didn't. But that didn't matter. Because it gave me the idea for the software I developed for pizzerias all over the world to automate and streamline their order-taking systems. I made my first billion before I was twenty-one."

"Wow" was all I could say.

"You know, Jimmy, I heard your pitch in there."

"You did?"

Mr. Grates nodded. "Those glass walls are pretty thin. You were kind of loud."

"Sorry about that."

"Don't be. You're just passionate about your idea. And you should be. I think it's fantastic! A book company run by kids that makes books for other kids? It's brilliant, Jimmy. Billion-dollar brilliant!"

Oh, boy.

I was getting excited.

I felt like my big break, my "Yes!" moment, was right around the corner. In fact, I could already picture it in my head.

Here you go, Jimmy. And if you need more cash, don't worry. There's plenty more where that came from.

All I had to do was smile and wait for Mr. Grates to make his billion-dollar offer.

"I wish I could've had your book company idea when I was a kid," said Mr. Grates. "But I didn't. You did. So I'd like to offer you something."

I swallowed hard. This was it. I knew it!

"Yes, sir?" I said.

"Jimmy, I want to offer you some advice: Never give up on your dream. Never, ever, *ever!* No matter what anybody says, no matter how loudly they laugh at you, keep on dreaming, Jimmy. Keep. On. Dreaming!"

"Yes, sir. I will. I promise."

"Okay. Great. Gotta go. Good luck, kid!"

And then he walked away.

Yep. I never, ever, *ever* saw that billionaire again.

So—how *did* I ever get this book company started?

You wouldn't believe it if I told you.

But I will anyway.

Chapter 33

Mission from Mars

Biking home, I took a shortcut through that park where (at least in my imagination) Quixote and I'd met those aliens.

So I couldn't help but remember what they'd told me. How we earthlings "must read more, and learn more, and think a whole lot more. Or else."

It definitely sounded like the planet was doomed and that it was partially my fault.

I had to fulfill my mission.

I had to start my book company and start making books for kids—especially the kids who don't really like books. I firmly believe that there's no such thing as a kid who hates reading. There are kids who *love* reading and kids who are reading the wrong books.

"The only books I read are the cheat guides to video games" is what this one guy at school (we'll call him X to protect his identity) always said.

"But X," I said, "reading will open up whole new worlds! Once you can read, you are forever free!"

"Who cares? And why are you calling me X, dude?"

That's when my newest friend and neighbor, Hailey, bopped up the hall. She was carrying a dog-eared copy of my *Alien Hunter* book. The edges of the pages were totally curled and crinkled.

"Here, X, read this." She handed him my book. "It's like a video game that takes place inside your brain. I've read it six times!"

"Are the graphics any good?" asked X.

"Sort of depends on your brain," said Hailey. "But I bet after you read the first chapter, you won't be able to put it down."

"You're on!" said X, grabbing the book, plopping down on the floor, and devouring it. (He was still sitting on the floor two hours later during the lunch stampede.)

That's when I remembered: Hailey still had all those copies of my Alien Hunter and Flying Mutant Children books stored in her parents' garage.

"By the way," she said, "I loved *Daniel Z* and *Maximum Flight*. Especially that character Max."

"Hey, are all those copies you hauled away still in good shape?"

"Of course. Our garage is an extremely awesome warehouse. There was one mouse, but he didn't seem interested in nibbling your books, just reading them."

"Huh?"

Hailey laughed. "I peeked through the window and it looked like the mouse was sitting on top of the stack of papers, reading your stories. And get this—the mouse looked blue. Bright blue."

A blue mouse who was freakishly intelligent and liked words?

If I may paraphrase Mark Twain, the mouse who does not read good books has no advantage over the mouse who cannot read them.

Hmmmmm.

Words from the Mouse would be a great title for a book.

Yep, I had another idea for my folder.

And another reason to open LOL Books ASAP!

Chapter 34

After-School Special Delivery

After school, I headed home with my neighbor Hailey.

You should see the mansion she lives in! I'm guessing it cost six bajillion dollars (I like stories more than doing math or estimating real estate prices). My first books were piled high inside the five-car garage, which currently only had three cars parked in it (I think they cost a bajillion dollars each, too).

"Dad sold his Lamborghini and bought a

motorcycle," said Hailey. "I think he's having a midlife crisis."

I nodded. I'd heard about those. That's when parents get to be like forty years old and decide to do something goofy like buy a sports car or quit their jobs. My parents hadn't had their midlife crises yet. Their jobs kept them too busy to even think about quitting them.

The blue mouse wasn't sitting on top of my stack of stories reading, but I could tell he *had* been.

"Gross," I said. "He pooped on the first page?"

"Yeah," said Hailey. "I don't get it. That's a real grabber of an opening. I dare anybody—human or rodent—to stop reading after that pie in the face!"

"Would you mind if I took a couple of these books home?" I asked, brushing the mouse droppings off the top of the heap.

"Of course not," said Hailey. "They're *your* stories. I'm just warehousing them until you get your book company going full time."

"Thanks. My neighbor, Maddie, needs a new read."

"So give her one of each. You'll still have two

dozen copies of each book you could sell or give away. Well, twenty-three clean copies. Looks like the mouse did some, uh, damage to the top copy of *Maximum Flight,* too."

Yes, there were tiny poop pellets decorating it.

"Critics," I said, shaking my head.

Anyway, I biked home with two books (clean copies from the middle of the piles) for Maddie to read. I put on a sterile mask (and washed my hands because: yuck!) before I went up to her room to deliver them.

"Is this the one about middle school and the boy who breaks all the rules?"

"No, we still don't have new copies of that one," I explained. "But these are sort of science-fictiony."

"Oooh," said Maddie. "I like science-fictiony books. I read that *Obsidian Blade* book you brought me from the library six times!"

Hailey had said the same thing about reading books "six times," so I made a mental note: When I started my book company, I had to make sure that every book I put out into the world was so good, kids would want to read it at least six times. I even thought about changing the name of my publishing company from Laugh Out Loud to Six Times Books. But then I thought too many kids would think I was giving them a multiplication problem with no answer.

After dropping off the fresh reads for Maddie, I went home, did my homework, fretted about that speech Mrs. Delvecchio could spring on me *any day,* and reread "The Raven" (a cool poem by Edgar Allan Poe). Then I brushed my teeth, went to bed, and basically couldn't fall asleep—not even when I dug out one of the boring books I keep on my bedside table for just such an emergency. (This one took seventeen pages to describe what was in a sandwich!)

I had what they call insomnia. It meant I couldn't sleep. Maybe it was because I was nervous about not flunking English. Or maybe I was worried about starting my book company without any money or investors. Or maybe I was freaked out by the strange noise coming from our garage.

It was an eerie, high-pitched wail.

Quixote heard it, too. He was lying at the foot of my bed with his ears perked up, whining.

Another screech followed the first. And then several more squeals and squawks.

I knew it couldn't be the cat.

We don't have one.

Chapter 35

Life Is but a Dream

The noises grew louder.

They started rushing on top of each other.

It sounded like demons screaming and wailing at each other.

"Quiet," I heard someone whisper. "You'll wake up Jimmy."

Oh, no. The demons knew my name.

The shrieking cries grew softer but they were still there.

I immediately knew what was going on. Our

garage had been invaded by evil duppies! A duppy is a type of ghost that roams the islands of Trinidad and Tobago late at night. My friend at school, Kenny Wilson, had heard all about them from his aunt Cherelle, who grew up in the Caribbean and loved to scare her nieces and nephews with folk-tales. Kenny says to keep the duppies out of your house, you need to sprinkle salt or rice all over the place because a duppy can't come into your dwelling until it's counted each individual grain.

Unfortunately, I hadn't sprinkled any salt in our driveway since the last time it snowed, and that was months ago.

Then I heard a tapping, as of someone gently rapping, rapping at my garage door. That's when I realized I should probably never read scary Edgar Allan Poe poems right before bedtime.

"Come on, Quixote," I said to my faithful canine companion. "We need to go sprinkle salt."

I swung my legs out of bed and slid my feet into my slippers. Quixote whimpered and tucked his head between his paws.

"Fine," I said. "I'll do this without you."

He merrily wagged his tail when I said that.

I tiptoed out of my bedroom (*without* my faithful canine companion), down the hall, and into the kitchen.

Slowly, very slowly, I creaked open the squeaky door that leads out to the garage.

I heard another screech. It was so shrill, it sent goose bumps shivering up my back and I realized why R. L. Stine named his spooky books after that particular spine-tingling sensation. Holding my breath and mustering all the courage I could, I pushed open the door.

Just as Mom plucked another note on an electric guitar.

"Mom?"

"Go back to bed, Jimmy," she said. "You're sleepwalking."

"No, I'm not," I said. "See? I have goose bumps on my arm."

"That's a very common side effect of sleep-walking," said Dad, who was also in the garage, sitting at some sort of angled table, drawing cartoons on a sketchpad. "Go back to bed, son."

This is all a dream, Jimmy. We're not even here. Neither is our electric guitar or drawing board.

I rubbed my eyes. They were both still there. Mom with her electric guitar, Dad with his drawing board.

"B-b-but," I stammered.

"Go to sleep," said Mom, trying her best to sound like a hypnotist. "You are sleepy, very sleepy."

"Go to bed," said Dad, "and you will receive your allowance five days early this week."

He handed me ten dollars.

I played along.

Clutching the cash, I raised both arms, zombie style, and turned around.

"I am sleepy, very sleepy..."

I Frankenstein-marched back to my bedroom, where I had a new question to ponder: Who were those two people in the garage and what had they done with my 'rents?

Chapter 36

A Winning Idea

The next morning, at breakfast, nobody said anything about the after-midnight weirdness in the garage.

I ate my cereal. Mom and Dad slurped coffee and nibbled PowerBars. There was no talk of garage-band guitar shredding or ninja warrior illustrations.

I headed to school with my crisp ten-dollar bill and made it through another English class without Mrs. Delvecchio calling on me to make an extemporaneous speech. Chris Grabbetts wasn't so lucky.

"Christopher?" said Mrs. Delvecchio. "Your speech, if you please."

Luckily, Chris was ready. He gave an impassioned plea for kids to be able to play the state lottery.

"They say the California State Lottery's mission is, and I quote, because I memorized it, Mrs. Delvecchio, they say the mission is to 'maximize supplemental funding for public education,' and yet they won't let anyone under the age of eighteen, who're almost all students, play it! How are we supposed to pay for college if we don't win the lottery? Why should we be forced to take out loans that will take years to pay off when all we really need to do is win at SuperLotto Plus or MEGA Millions?"

"Or," Chris continued, "how about that Set For Life scratch-off game? You give me twenty thousand dollars a month for twenty-five years, I could get a PhD degree! Maybe. Sometimes those things take *twenty-six* years."

It was a good speech. Mrs. Delvecchio gave Chris a B-minus because, even though it was filled with facts and well argued, she didn't want to "condone underage gambling."

"It's not gambling!" Chris protested. "It's all about kids and schools!"

"Would you like me to change that B-minus to a C, Mr. Grabbetts?"

"No, ma'am."

Hearing Chris's speech gave me a great idea.

"I know how we're going to fund Laugh Out Loud Books," I told everybody after school.

"How?" asked all my buddies.

I waved my Hamilton in the air. (A Hamilton is like ten percent of a Benjamin.)

I believe in my dream so I'm gonna invest in it. I am not throwing away my shot!

"I'm going to win the lottery!"

"Huh?"

"The Powerball jackpot is now one hundred and forty-eight million dollars," I said. "All I have to do is match the numbers on five white balls and the red Powerball. I do that—BOOM! We're in business."

"You realize," said Pierce, our resident brainiac, "that the odds of you winning are one in two hundred and ninety-two million, two hundred and one thousand, three hundred and thirty-eight?"

"Okay. But what are the odds of someone else winning it?"

Pierce blinked. "Um, one in two hundred and ninety-two million, two hundred and one thousand, three hundred and thirty-eight."

"See? They have terrible odds, so I have a shot."

"Small problem," said Maxine. "How are you going to buy the ticket? You're not eighteen."

"Easy," I said with a grin. "Tailspin Tommy."

Chapter 37

Tommy Time

Thomas Kipplemeyer is the big brother of Bob and Abby Kipplemeyer, the twins who live down the street from me.

Thomas is nineteen, which means he can buy a Powerball ticket in the state of California. The twins call Thomas Tailspin Tommy because, well, let's just say he's always falling helplessly in love with every pretty girl he meets. Even the ones he meets in perfume ads. He spends most of his time flirting with girls or scrunching his hair (so he can flirt with girls). I figured he could buy my Power-ball ticket for me.

Especially if I take him to Pizza 1, the convenience store over on First Street.

The cashier who sells the Powerball tickets is a very pretty girl named Angelika.

The instant Tommy saw Angelika behind the pizza counter, he agreed to help me out. I also promised to pay him one percent of my winnings as a service fee.

The Powerball tickets cost two dollars each. With my ten dollars, I had five chances to win!

"Here you go, Jimmy," said Tailspin Tommy as he strolled out of Pizza 1 and handed me my ticket to becoming a multimillionaire. "I gave her your numbers. And guess what?"

"What?"

He winked at me. "She gave me *her* number, too! I think it's my new body spray. The ladies can't resist it."

Score! I had my winning lottery ticket! Laugh Out Loud Books' future was secure.

Okay, that was dumb, right?

I mean, who actually wins Powerball?

But then I started thinking about *Holes* by Louis Sachar. It's one of my favorite books. I love how Stanley Yelnats and his new friend Zero (spoiler alert) find the Kissing Bandit's treasure at the end of the book. Stanley's family has been cursed with bad luck ever since his great-great-grandfather stole a pig from Madame Zeroni. Stanley breaks the curse and his luck changes.

I had a feeling my luck was about to change, too!

The next Powerball drawing would be televised live on Saturday night at 10:59 p.m. At 11 p.m., I planned on being a newly minted multimillionaire who could self-finance my book business.

When I showed the gang my tickets, they all chanted, "Jimmy's gonna win! Jimmy's gonna win! Jimmy's gonna win!"

"If I win," I told them, "you guys win, too! I'll use all the money to build the Laugh Out Loud Book Company's first factory and warehouse."

"Will it have a Ferris wheel?" asked Rafe.

"You bet. The jackpot this week just went up to one hundred and seventy-five million dollars. We can have *two* Ferris wheels!"

My bold prediction earned me more cheers and chants.

Hey, you never know, as they used to say in Lotto commercials.

I mean, technically, I had a chance at winning.

Dreams do come true, especially in books. Especially the ones filled with fairy tales.

Jiminy Cricket even sings about it happening to Pinocchio. Okay, that's a movie, not a book, but you know, "When You Wish Upon a Star" and all that.

I just hoped it wouldn't be cloudy Saturday night.

I needed to find a star to wish on around 10:58 p.m.

Chapter 38

My Lucky Night?

Okay, I knew it was a long shot, but I was starting to get excited about winning Powerball!

So were my friends.

"You're living my dream, man," said Chris Grabbetts.

"Hey," I said to him. "You're the one who gave me the idea. With your speech."

"Guess you'll have to send Tommy Kipplemeyer in to collect your prize. You probably have to be eighteen or older to win, too."

"Yeah. I guess so."

And then I started thinking about all the detective books I've read where greed turns people into "dirty double-crossers."

Would Tailspin Tommy do that to me?

My lottery tickets were getting kind of grubby and crinkly because I kept taking them out of my pocket to stare at them. I was so nervous, I was afraid I might rub all the numbers off.

Meanwhile, since it was a Saturday, Mom and Dad were actually home. But instead of doing paperwork like they did most weekends, Mom was jamming on her electric guitar again and Dad was drawing more ninja warriors on his sketchpad.

Neither of them knew, but I was peeking at them through a crack in the garage door.

What are they up to? I wondered. *Have they finally found time to have their midlife crises?*

For the longest time, my parents didn't have hobbies or interests. They had jobs.

I was about to barge in and ask them what the heck was going on. But I was too nervous.

It was Powerball day!

Hailey had invited everybody to her house to watch the big drawing. Her parents have a TV the size of a minivan. Seriously. It takes up an entire wall. They also have a popcorn cart. Have I mentioned that they're bajillionaires?

(Yes, I had thought about asking Hailey's mom and dad for a loan to start my book company, but Hailey advised against it. "They'd want total control," she said. "Plus, they'd force you to write books about algorithms and nanocircuits.")

My parents didn't mind that I was heading down the block at ten thirty at night to watch TV with my friends. It wasn't a school night and they were still in the garage doing secret weird stuff with guitars and sketchpads.

"This is it," said Kenny, his mouth full of popcorn. "Your last day as a nonmillionaire."

"You'll be as rich as Steve Grates," joked Maxine.

"Hardly," I said. "Besides—I don't really want to be rich. I just want to open up my book company!"

"Quiet, you guys," said Chris. "Here it comes!"

At exactly 10:59, a guy in a tuxedo started reading numbered Ping-Pong balls as they popped out of a clear hopper and into what looked like a gerbil tube.

Finally, one red ball shot out of a second hopper and rolled into the Powerball gerbil tube.

The whole thing was over in thirty seconds.

Aaaaand…

Drumroll, please!

I didn't win.

In fact, not a single one of the numbers on my tickets ended up in the gerbil tubes.

What are the odds of that?

(I didn't say it out loud or Pierce would've told me.)

Well, that's what happened. My numbers were totally unlucky.

So I didn't start my book company by winning Powerball.

Chapter 39

Web Browsing

Whatever was going on in the garage was having a strange effect on both of my parents.

They were starting to pay attention to me (when they weren't rehearsing guitar riffs or sketching ninja avengers).

I was in my bedroom, searching the Web on my computer, when my dad knocked on my open door and asked me, "What are you doing, Jimmy?"

"Not giving up," I answered, because I was still searching for a way to financially kick-start my dream.

"You do that a lot, don't you?" said Dad.

"I have a dream," I told him. "You should never give up on your dreams."

Dad looked like I'd just given him something to think about. Or gas. Then he strolled away.

I realized I needed my own rags-to-riches story. Something like *Ready Player One* by Ernest Cline, which takes place in 2045 and is all about an incredible, hyperrealistic, 3-D online gaming world called the OASIS and a race to win billions. I needed to become teenager Wade Watts and hunt down the Easter egg hidden inside the OASIS by its whack-aloon creator so I could become the richest kid on the planet.

Somehow, some way, I was going to launch my book company.

I started a new Google search: "NEED MONEY FOR START-UP."

The second hit was an interesting ad:

Money for Start Up!
$5,000–$500,000. 2-Hour Approval.

Whoa!

The Internet wanted to give me half a million dollars and it would only take two hours? I was all in!

I clicked on the link.

A testimonial video opened on my screen. It was a young woman, maybe twenty-five.

"Hi! I would, like, so totally recommend this amazing Internet company to anyone in the start-up phase of building their business. I was approved in two hours and received all the funding I needed in just two weeks."

Okay, I thought. *I could wait two weeks.*

"Now," the video clip lady continued, "my

business is up and running and booming. I would totally recommend Startup Loan Sharks to anyone like me who never reads the fine print and doesn't realize that the Sharks will be charging me fifty percent interest compounded every fourteen hours for the next thirty years, whatever the heck that means."

I didn't understand what it meant either, so I started filling in the boxes.

Name. Address. Date of birth.

When I entered my birthday information, my computer made a funny BLOOP-BLOOP-BLOOP squiggly noise, like I'd just lost a video game.

My screen went blank.

Then type scrolled across my screen:

THIS SITE ISN'T FOR KIDS, KID.
CONTACT US AGAIN WHEN YOU TURN 21.
NOW GO EAT YOUR VEGETABLES AND LEAVE US ALONE.
YOU REALLY THOUGHT SOMEONE WOULD LOAN SERIOUS
MONEY TO A GOOFY KID LIKE YOU?
HA! HA!

The scrolling type disappeared and emoticons danced across my computer.

You guessed it.

Some more grown-ups were laughing out loud at me.

Chapter 40

Money Man to the Rescue!

There were 38,400,000 other results for my Google search of "need money for start-up."

I checked out a few more. They all laughed out loud at me, too.

I started scribbling "Ha, Ha" on a notepad.

Then I wrote *Jimmy Ha-Ha,* which I thought might make a good title for a book someday—*if* I ever found someone to give me money for my start-up. I tore the *Jimmy Ha-Ha* page off the pad and stuffed it into my bulging idea folder.

I don't know about you, but whenever I'm feeling kind of weak and powerless, I reach for my pile of comic books. I imagine myself as one of the heroes. Maybe I'm the Flash and can run really fast. Maybe I'm Superman and I can fly. Maybe I'm the Incredible Hulk and all I have to do is get mad to become super strong.

But what if...

Yes, I was having another brainstorm.

What if I could become Money Man?

I would be a new kind of superhero. All the bullies at school would think I was a mild-mannered chess-playing nerd. But then I'd slip into my locker and change into my green superhero outfit and become Money Man. My cape would be a hundred-dollar bill the size of a beach towel. The eyeholes in my mask would be silver dollars with the centers cut out. And instead of sticky spiderwebs, streams of cash would come shooting out of my wrists! I'd be a superpowered ATM, dispensing money wherever it was needed. First I'd start up my business with a mountain of moola and then I'd fly around like an airborne Robin Hood raining cash on poor people around the globe. And I wouldn't have to rob from the rich because, like I said, Money Man can make money with a flick of his wrist.

Too bad I didn't have a secret identity as a moneymaking superhero. I stayed up super late brainstorming, but no matter how hard I tried, I couldn't imagine my way into a book company.

Once again, around midnight, I was serenaded by a wailing guitar solo. Only this time, it sounded closer.

The living room.

Quixote was definitely interested. Probably because Mom was practicing her high notes. I'm sure they hurt the dog's ears even worse than they hurt mine.

We both hurried out of the bedroom to see what was going on.

"I'm not sleepwalking," I announced when I entered the room where Mom was strumming her guitar and Dad was drawing more ninjas. "I'm not sleep–dog-walking, either. What the heck is going on around here?"

Mom smiled. Dad, too.

"We're giving you the garage, Jimmy," said Mom.

"It's yours," added Dad. "For your dream. Your book company."

Quixote cocked his head and gave a questioning whine.

Me too, Quixote.

"You inspire us, Jimmy," explained Dad. "Your perseverance in the face of overwhelming disappointment, disaster, failure—"

"Not to mention ridicule," said Mom.

"Right," said Dad. "That too. Your grit, determination, and stick-to-itiveness—"

"Is that a word, Jimmy?" asked Mom. "Stick-to-itiveness."

"It's in the dictionary," I said.

"See?" said Dad. "You're a natural-born wordsmith. So never, never, never give up, son. Follow your dream. The way you have inspired others to follow theirs."

"Others?" I said. "Like who?"

"Us," said Mom.

"The garage is yours, Jimmy," said Dad. "We're parking the cars on the street. Do whatever you need to make your dream come true!"

"Um, okay."

"But," Mom added, "I'll need the garage for a couple of hours every Wednesday."

"Huh?"

"That's when my new band is going to rehearse."

Chapter 41

Garage Bands

Well, that was a nice surprise.

Not just that Mom and Dad were letting me have the garage for Laugh Out Loud Books (except for Wednesdays between 6 and 8 p.m.). I was also pleasantly surprised to learn that Mom and Dad still had dreams of their own.

Seems Dad had always wanted to illustrate graphic novels and manga comics. So he went to the art store and bought a drawing board, a gooseneck lamp, some fancy paper, and a ton of markers.

Mom, it turns out, had wanted to play lead guitar in a rock band since she was twelve. Maybe someday, her dream will come true. Maybe on Wednesdays. Although I heard Mom and her friends rehearsing once. Their band doesn't have a name yet but I have a suggestion: the Pretty Awful But Not Completely Terribly Bad Band.

"This is so cool," said Chris Grabbetts when he came over to check out the Laugh Out Loud Book Company setup in my garage. "We're going to be like Steve Jobs and Steve Wozniak. They started Apple Computer in a garage, way back in 1975. You can call me Woz."

"How about I call you Grabs instead?"

"Perfect!"

Our book-making factory/warehouse wasn't much, but it was a start. We had a computer, a printer, and a carton of copy paper that Dad picked up at the office supplies store and wrapped with a big red ribbon and bow.

"Fill these pages with your dreams, son!" he said when he gave me the gift, which, by the way, weighed a ton.

Hailey, with the help of the whole gang, wheeled those books we'd been storing in her garage over to my garage.

"Um, the mouse flipped through the pages and pooped on the last chapters of both books, too."

"I guess you can't please everyone," I muttered.

"No," said Hailey. "I think, with mice, pooping all over your work is considered a compliment. It's like they're marking their territory. Claiming and acclaiming your work."

"Huh," I said with a shrug. "Works for me."

With everything in place and my bulging idea folder practically bursting at the seams, I started imagining that my life would soon turn into a rags-to-riches story, like something out of a Charles Dickens novel!

But then Grabs brought me crashing back to reality.

"So, uh, now what do we do? Write more books?"

"No," said Hailey. "First, we need to make the company's books look better."

"I could draw cover art," said Rafe.

"That's not what I mean," said Hailey. "We need to put some money in the Laugh Out Loud bank account."

"How?" I asked. "I spent my last unexpected windfall on losing Powerball tickets."

"Easy," said Hailey. She gestured toward the stack of books. "We roll up the garage door and have a book sale!"

Chapter 42

Garage/ Book Sale

It was a glorious Sunday afternoon, so we went to work!

Rafe, with a little help from fellow artist Dad, did some quick GARAGE/BOOK SALE signs. We spread out around the neighborhood and posted them on telephone poles and NO PARKING signposts.

We arranged the copies of my first books on our patio table, which we hauled out of the backyard. Then Mom brewed a big pot of coffee.

"You can't run a proper bookstore without coffee," she said. "Plus, you can charge for it."

"Hey, Jimmy?" said Chris.

"Yeah?"

"I'm on the staff, right?"

"Definitely, Grabs."

"Cool."

Then he whipped up a quick sign on the cardboard backing from one of Mom's yellow legal pads. He scrawled STAFF PICK in big letters on it and stuck the sign in front of the piles of my titles.

Our driveway bookshop was open for business.

Pretty soon, we were racking up the sales.

And get this, some people wanted me to autograph their books!

"You're going to be a famous author someday," one lady told me. "This will be worth a million dollars!"

"If it is," I told her, "could you loan me half a million? I want to open a real book company with a factory that has a water slide and a Ferris wheel."

She just sort of grinned and patted me on the head. "Of course you do."

We didn't have a "suggested cover price" like most "real" books do. We just told our customers

to suggest a price. Most gave us like twenty or twenty-five dollars. A couple of kids gave us fifty cents. Hey, it was everything they had and they were the ones we were actually writing the books for.

"You know if you keep doing that you'll go broke, right?" asked Maxine.

"Yeah. But I like giving stuff away almost as much as I like making books."

"You're an odd duck, Jimmy. An extremely odd duck."

"I know. But the odd ducks are the most interesting ones, don't you think?"

Around noon, when the books were almost all gone, Mom added a line of baked goods to her coffee shop: chewy chocolate chip cookies. From a tube.

"I feel like Starbucks," she said. "Does anybody want a Grande No Foam Mocha Frappa Whip A Chino Amotiado Tazo Drip?"

"No, ma'am," said everybody.

"Good. Because I have no idea how to make one."

At two o'clock, all our books were gone. Plus,

Mom had sold a ton of coffee and chocolate chip cookies.

"How much did we make?" asked Hailey.

"Four hundred and fifty-three dollars and twenty-five cents," reported Dad, who'd been manning the money box for us.

"That's enough to make more copies of the Middle School book!" said Rafe. "We can run them off at the copy shop and have another garage/book sale next weekend!"

It was an awesome idea.

Until Monday afternoon, when, all of a sudden, it wasn't.

Chapter 43

Meeting Uncle Sam

Two guys in dark suits came knocking on our front door Monday around six o'clock in the evening.

Remarkably, both Mom and Dad were home.

In fact, they'd both been home all day. Dad had some ninja warriors he wanted to finish inking in. Mom said she was "this close" to nailing her "Stairway to Heaven" solo—whatever that meant.

In other words, major plot twist, neither one of them went to work for the first time since I've known them, which, of course, is all of my life!

"You're our inspiration, Jimmy," said Dad. "We've been ignoring our dreams for so long we almost forgot we had them."

"Thank you for this gift, Jimmy," said Mom. "Without your example, I never would have unleashed my inner Jimi Hendrix."

I had absolutely no idea what that meant, either, but I was happy to see them both so happy.

On the other hand, I wasn't so happy to see both the guys in the suits smiling, especially when one of them said, "I'm here on behalf of Uncle Sam."

(I never realized I had an uncle named Sam.)

"Now then," said the Uncle Sam man with a sinister smile, "exactly how much money did you make at your book sale yesterday?"

I answered before Mom could raise her hand to shush me: "Four hundred and fifty-three dollars and twenty-five cents."

"My client refuses to answer any further questions," said Mom, holding up her hand to silence me.

"I'm your client?" I say. "Cool!"

"Ma'am," said the man, "by refusing to answer, your son here could be in serious violation of the Internal Revenue Service rules and regulations."

"The IRS?" snapped Dad. "You guys are with the IRS?"

"He is," said the other guy. "I'm with the city of San Jose. To operate a business in our jurisdiction, your son will need a permit."

"And you will need to pay taxes on any income your ongoing book sales continue to generate," said the IRS guy.

"And the local sales tax," said the city guy. "Don't forget the local sales tax."

"What you did in your driveway this weekend,"

explained the IRS man, "is illegal unless you fill out the proper paperwork."

"Fine," said Mom, shifting into her barracuda lawyer mode. "We will endeavor to adhere to all local, state, and federal ordinances associated with Laugh Out Loud Books, LLC."

"I'm an LLC?" I asked.

"You will be," said Mom.

"Awesome. What does it mean?"

"That to keep your dream alive, you're going to need to file all sorts of paperwork," said Dad. "Good thing your mother and I have so much practice filling out forms."

"Totally," said Mom, pumping her fist in the air like the heavy metal rocker she dreamed of becoming.

"And," said the city guy, pulling out a photo of Mom and Chris G. pouring coffee into cups, "if you continue to sell hot beverages and cookies at your book sales, you need to contact the California state health inspectors. Have them come by. Check your kitchen and serving areas for violations, such as rodent droppings."

Great.

I just hoped the mouse from Hailey's garage didn't decide to move down the street to ours!

Chapter 44

Don't Quit Your Day Job?

Mom and Dad stayed home from work for another day.

"We read your books," Mom said when I came home from school.

"They're quite good," added Dad.

"Um, how could you read them?" I asked. "We sold out all the copies and now we have to pay all those taxes and fees. So we don't have enough money to print more copies."

"Yes, we do!" said Mom. "Your father and I cashed in our savings account."

"What?"

"We believe in your dream, Jimmy," said Dad. "We're just sorry we didn't believe in it sooner."

"So we printed out fresh copies of all three books from your computer," said Mom.

"They're real page-turners, son," said Dad. "Even though you wrote them for kids, we couldn't put 'em down!"

"And," said Mom, "we're going to fight all this tax nonsense."

"What's next?" said Dad. "Is the government going to start taxing lemonade stands?"

"How dare they try to crush your entrepreneurial spirit!" said Mom.

"We'll clean out all our bank accounts to fight them if we have to!" shouted Dad.

"The IRS shall feel our wrath!" added Mom.

With Mom and Dad's money from the bank, we were able to fill the garage with fresh copies of my first three books.

My 'rents also totally stopped going to their offices.

"We have all sorts of vacation days saved up," said Mom.

"Because both of us worked so hard, neither one of us even thought about taking a vacation," added Dad.

It's true. My trip to Legoland? I went with Chris Grabbetts and his family.

Mom and Dad stayed home for the rest of the week and used their paperwork skills to file everything we needed to make Laugh Out Loud an official business. We framed our brand-new license and hung it up in the garage. The state health inspector gave Mom's coffeemaker an A. I went around the neighborhood and hung up more signs.

BIG BOOK SALE

SATURDAY AT 10 AM
PRESENTED BY
LAUGH OUT LOUD
BOOKS LLC.
YOU PAY US. WE PAY TAXES.

Saturday came. The gang assembled in the garage.

"Look at all those books!" exclaimed Maxine, marveling at the mountain of newly printed manuscripts stacked up in tidy columns towering ten feet high.

"My mom and dad basically cashed in their life savings to make more copies," I explained.

"You think they might've gone a little overboard?" asked Pierce. "There has to be a thousand books in here."

"Nine hundred and ninety-nine," said Dad. "Three hundred and thirty-three copies each of Jimmy's first three titles."

"But," said Chris, "we've been selling two or three at a time. Maybe a couple dozen. Why do we need like a thousand books?"

"We call it inventory," said Dad proudly.

"Go big or stay home," said Mom. "Right, Jimmy?"

Oops. She must've heard me say that after I heard Hailey say it.

"Let's open the doors," said Dad. "It's time to sell some books."

He busily thumbed a remote. The metal door rumbled up.

Sheets of rain started blowing sideways into the garage.

I think San Jose, California, was having its first-ever typhoon!

Chapter 45

Rain, Rain, Go Away

It rained harder.

The howling wind grew fiercer. We were all getting wetter.

So were my books!

It was like Mother Nature had a fire hose trained on our wide-open garage door and wasn't afraid to spray us with it.

"Close the door!" I shouted.

"No way," said Dad, the guy holding the remote. "If we close our doors, our customers won't be able to find us."

"And," said Mom, screaming to be heard over the sideways torrent of rainwater pelting her in the face, "if our customers can't find us, they can't buy books! It's Basic Business 101, Jimmy."

"Nobody's going to go book-shopping in a monsoon!" I shouted over the gale-force winds. "Close the door! The books are getting drenched!"

One important lesson I learned that Saturday? Books don't sell very well in the rain. Except, of course, in Seattle, which is a great book town *because* of all the rain. Reading a good book gives you something to do on dark and dreary days. But bookstores in Seattle don't make customers shop in an open-air bazaar in the middle of a sideways thunderstorm.

When Dad finally gave in and closed the garage doors, our towering heaps of books looked more like melting snowmen. Wilted pages were glued together. The manuscripts were soggier than soaked sponges. The pages were wrinkled beyond recognition.

We shouldn't've gone big. We should've stayed home.

I've heard about plot wrinkles, but this is ridiculous.

When the sun finally came out the next day, we loaded the soaked heaps of worthless paper into recycling bins and pushed them out to the curb.

"At least we won't have to pay any taxes this week," said Dad.

"And," said Mom, "the garage will be nice and empty for band practice on Wednesday."

That's when things got even worse.

Sunday night Mom and Dad both received telephone calls.

From their bosses.

"We heard the IRS paid you a visit," Dad's boss told him. "We're certified public accountants. We do people's taxes. We can't have employees with children who try to cheat the tax code. If word of your son's tax-avoidance schemes were to leak, we'd lose all our clients. We cannot take that risk. You're fired!"

Mom's call was basically the same. "You're a tax attorney!" her boss hollered over the phone. "Your son can't antagonize the IRS! If he does, the IRS will come after all our clients!"

She was fired, too.

"On the bright side," said Dad, sounding sort of shocked, "now we both have all the time in the world to pursue our dreams."

"Rock on," said Mom, limply pumping her fist halfway up into the air.

I could tell they were both feeling lost. Everything that was secure in their lives had just been ripped away.

Things were so sad around our house that night, I considered changing the name of my book company from Laugh Out Loud to Weeping in Agony.

But then I had a better idea.

I realized it was time for me to call it quits.

Chapter 46

Stick a Fork in Me, I'm Done

Remember how this whole book company idea was supposed to be fun?

Well, now, instead of water slides coursing through a fun factory, we had water sliding into the garage, destroying months of work. Instead of a Ferris wheel, we had the wheels on trash barrels filled with water-damaged manuscripts.

And then there were the taxes and the licenses and the fees and my parents losing their jobs.

I wondered why I'd ever dreamed this impossible

dream. (Maybe because I named my dog Quixote? After all, that was a guy who did not know when to quit.)

"Worst. Idea. Ever," I said to myself when I was alone in my room. (Mom and Dad had, more or less, commandeered the family room so they could stare blankly at the TV and mutter, "What have we done?" over and over and over again.)

I picked up my idea folder. It was six inches thick.

Which made it kind of hard to stuff into the trash can.

But stuff it I did.

Good-bye to all the dozens of little ideas that I turned into one colossally bad idea.

Since the idea folder basically took up my entire wastebasket, I marched out to the curb to dump it into the recycling bin.

"So long, Laugh Out Loud Books," I said, putting an end to my crazy idea. "Now I understand why all those grown-ups laughed at me and my nutso idea. They were right. It was laughable. *I'm* laughable."

I'd let down all my friends. I'd cost my parents their jobs. I'd missed soccer practice for months. (Yeah. I used to play—before I got too busy thinking about books to even think about doing anything else.)

And why?

Because my next-door neighbor Maddie had said, "Give me another book, Jimmy. Please?"

I still might give her another book. But if I did, it would come from the library, not some pie-in-the-sky book factory.

On Monday, I headed straight to the library during my flex period.

Writing is never a sure thing. But reading always is.

When Ms. Sprenkle saw how down I was, she suggested I read a book called *Hatchet* by Gary Paulsen. It's all about a thirteen-year-old boy named Brian from New York City who crash-lands in a lake when the pilot of the small plane he's flying in (it's a tiny prop plane; the kind without a copilot) has a heart attack and dies. Brian, the city kid, is on his own in the wilderness, with nothing but his hatchet. Think *Survivor* but for real. While hunting on the edge of the lake, Brian senses something is watching him. It's a wolf, "not as big as a bear but somehow seeming that large."

Now, I have to admit something.

While reading *Hatchet,* I fell asleep. Not because Mr. Paulsen's book was boring. No way. It's still one of the most exciting adventure tales ever written. I think I was drowsy because I didn't sleep at all the night before. I'd been too busy thinking about how stupid I'd been.

Anyway, snoozing there in the library, I had a dream that I was raised in the wilderness by wolves. And the wolves were all big readers. In my dream, the wolves lectured me about the importance of books. They told me that one day I'd start my own book company.

I told the wolves I had already tried (repeatedly) to make a book company and failed.

That's when a wolf that looked a lot like Yoda showed up. He said, "There is no try, only do."

I woke up mumbling, "A wolf never quits and a quitter never wolfs."

I didn't know what it meant.

Until I saw Maddie.

Chapter 47

Keep Hope Alive

Believe it or not, the girl who could never leave her own house walked into the middle school library!

Her little brother, Sammy, was with her.

"Hiya, Jimmy!" she said.

"What are you doing here?"

"Our first field trip," said Sammy.

"I wanted to see the place with all the books," said Maddie. "The ones you've been bringing me all these years."

"She's been having some really good days lately," explained Sammy. "Her doctor gave her permission to go outside!"

"For a couple of hours, anyway," said Maddie.

"That's great!" I said. "What happened to change your doc's mind?"

Maddie grinned. "I think I wore him down. I wouldn't quit bugging him about it. I wouldn't give up hope. And it was all because of that book you brought me."

"Um, which one?"

She pointed at the table where *Hatchet* lay open.

"The exact same one *you're* reading. You brought it home to me a couple of months ago."

"I did?"

"Yep. And I totally memorized my favorite passage."

"She did," said Sammy, rolling his eyes. "She repeats it to me all the time."

"It's when the hero realizes he'd forgotten to think about the rescuers who might be searching for him." Maddie cleared her throat and started reciting her favorite lines: "'He had to keep thinking of them because if he forgot them and did not think of them they might forget about him. And he had to keep hoping. He had to keep hoping.'" She smiled. "I needed to do the same thing. To keep hoping. Thanks for that, Jimmy. Oh, look! A whole wall of books I haven't read yet."

"You only have thirty more minutes," said Sammy. "Doctor's orders."

"Next time, I hope I'll get to stay outside even longer, Jimmy."

"Yeah," I said. "I hope so, too."

Sammy and Maddie hurried off to find Ms. Sprenkle so they could check out some more books.

It's amazing what you can learn from a good book.

Or from someone who's read one.

Seeing Maddie living her dream, I realized that if I kept hope alive, maybe, just maybe, I could still make my dream come true, too!

Maybe I could still start a book company.

Maybe I didn't need physical copies of my books (which had all been sold or destroyed). Maybe I didn't even need an idea folder, which I'd tossed into the trash.

Maybe all I really needed was HOPE and one lucky break!

Before the day was over, I had both!

Chapter 48

My Lucky Day

When I biked home from school that afternoon, guess who was standing in my driveway?

Hailey, from down the block.

She was cradling something in her arms.

My idea folder.

At my old school, I won a gold medal for Dumpster diving.

"You know, Jimmy," she said, shaking her head and laughing, "you always seem to throw out the most incredible stuff. The ideas in this folder are amazing. The robots and the kid who becomes a superhero and the treasure-hunting family and the mouse who saves *his* whole family and Rafe spending the worst years of his life in middle school and the girl everybody calls Jacky Ha-Ha." She took a quick breath. "But my absolute favorite idea is the one about the funny comedian kid in the wheelchair."

"Yeah," I said. "Jamie Grimm. He never gives up."

"Exactly!" said Hailey. "And neither should you."

"I know. But nobody wants to give me the seed money I need to launch my start-up."

"Oh, yes they do," said Hailey. "You just haven't met them yet."

"I've tried."

Hailey pulled a business card out of her pocket. Handed it to me.

"Try again."

"Who's this?"

"Friends of my parents. *Super-wealthy* friends. I would've told you about them sooner but they were on this three-month-long vacation over in Nepal studying mindfulness with a mystic on top of a mountain. They're kind of eccentric."

"Eccentric?"

"You know—bizarre, unconventional, weird. They have to be approached in just the right way."

I studied the card.

"So," said Hailey. "They just got back from Asia. You want to try pitching them?"

I shook my head. "No. I don't want to 'try.' I want to DO it!"

Chapter 49

Who Is Y?

Hailey and I headed into the garage and fired up the computer.

"If we're going to pitch Mr. and Mrs. Y, we need to know everything there is to know about them," I said.

"Totally," said Hailey. "For instance, did you know they're the ones who bought my parents' start-up for a bajillion dollars?"

"No," I admitted. "I did not know that."

Hailey clicked and clacked computer keys,

calling up more searches on the Ys. "Their real last name is Yingerlinger."

"I can see why they go with just the Y," I said.

"Just last year, before flying to Nepal, Mr. Yingerlinger swam across San Francisco Bay from Alcatraz Island all the way to Aquatic Park in Berkeley. And he wasn't wearing a wet suit. Just SpongeBob swim trunks. Meanwhile, Mrs. Yingerlinger runs a university for entrepreneurs where part of the graduation ceremony is jumping off a trampoline into a bin of Nerf balls."

"This is cool," I said, calling up a search of my own on my smartphone. "It says, 'Mr. and Mrs. Yingerlinger prefer moon shots to slow and steady slogs up a hill.'"

"It's true," said Hailey. "They love crazy big ideas. Like flying cars, grocery stores that grow their own corn…"

"Seriously?"

"Hey, they have all those long aisles. Why not plant rows of corn?"

"Oh-kay."

"They're also big on discovering new ways to save pollinating bees without getting stung!"

"So," I said, really starting to believe in my dream again, "they might love a book company for kids run by kids! Especially if we add a trampoline and a bin of Nerf balls to our factory floor plan."

We set to work.

Rafe came over and drew up new blueprints for our book company. He put the trampoline right next to the roller coaster. Maxine and Chris helped me flesh out a few of the ideas in my folder. Maddie sent her brother, Sammy, over with a plate of freshly baked chocolate chip cookies.

"She went shopping for the ingredients herself," Sammy told us. "Her doctor is letting her spend up to two hours a day outside the house now. Maddie hopes it will be three soon!"

Pierce, Kenny, and Hailey put together a Power-Point presentation because, apparently, you can't have a business meeting without one of those.

We were all set to go!

"So," asked Chris, "where exactly are Mr. and Mrs. Yingerlinger's offices?"

Good question.

One that Hailey and I hadn't researched yet.

But then we did.

"Their headquarters is all the way up in Marin County," reported Hailey glumly. "A two-hour-and-four-minute drive."

"Unless you have a flying car," said Chris. "Then it would probably take an hour, maybe less."

"How long is the walk?" asked Maxine. "Because, sorry, Jimmy, you're not old enough to drive. Or fly."

And just like that, all the new air went out of my big idea balloon again.

Until Mom and Dad stepped into the garage.

"It's such a beautiful day outside," said Mom.

"We know you kids are busy in here, chasing after your dreams and all," said Dad. "But even the most enterprising entrepreneurs need to take a break now and then. Whaddya say, Jimmy? Wanna go for a ride?"

"Yes!" I said. "Right now! To Marin County! And these guys are all coming with us!"

Chapter 50

Hit the Road, Jimmy!

Before we all piled into the minivan, Maxine told me I needed to go inside and change my clothes.

"You should dress like an author," she said. "You know. Tweed jacket. Ascot."

"What's an ascot?" asked Chris.

"It's like a silk scarf, only smaller."

"I don't have an ascot," I explained.

"You should look hipper than tweed," said Hailey. "Remember, the Yingerlingers are eccentric and kooky. I read somewhere that Mr.

Yingerlinger hasn't worn a business suit or a necktie in two decades. And Mrs. Yingerlinger prefers yoga clothes."

I nodded. "Probably better for the trampoline."

After some more debate, it was agreed (by everybody except me) that I should go for the full Neil Gaiman look: black leather jacket, black T-shirt, black jeans, slightly rumpled hair. (They also wanted me to grow some beard stubble, but that wasn't going to happen anytime soon.)

"You guys?" I said, combing my hair with my hand. "This doesn't feel right. If I'm going in there to ask a pair of bazillionaires to back me, I need to *be* me. Just straight-up Jimmy, plain and simple."

"Not to be confused with Sarah, plain and tall," cracked Hailey.

Anyway, I took off all that black and put on my usual sweater and lucky scarf. Even though it was seventy and sunny. Okay, maybe I already *do* dress like an eccentric author and just never realized it.

Wardrobe crisis over, we all squeezed into our minivan. Mom drove, Dad argued with the GPS lady's directions.

Then it got worse: Mom made us listen to jam bands all the way from San Jose to Marin County.

"This next guitar solo should cover fifty miles," she said when a new Grateful Dead tune started playing.

Apparently, the Grateful Dead were big stars in the Bay Area, back in the days when people had an entire hour to listen to one song.

Finally, we arrived in lush and bucolic Marin County. By the way, *bucolic* is one of those writerly words that I probably shouldn't use because if I do, everybody, adults included, will have to go find a dictionary and look it up, which means they might miss the rest of my story. I should probably just tell you Marin County has a lot of very beautiful countryside filled with soft green hills.

And the Yingerlingers had an eighty-acre "ranch" for "growing ideas" smack-dab in the middle of it.

"This is so amazing!" I said. "I can't wait till we meet the Yingerlingers!"

"So," asked Dad, checking his watch. "When's your appointment, Jimmy?"

Ooops.

Guess what else Hailey and I forgot to do?

Chapter 51

My Dream Destination

Okay. We probably should've phoned ahead, but we didn't.

"You don't have an appointment?" said Mom. "Bummer."

Yes, ever since she quit her day job, she was sounding more and more like a hip rock star.

"Guess we could go back home and drive up here again tomorrow," suggested Dad. "If, you know, they give you an appointment."

"No!" I said, and not just because I couldn't

stand another long van ride listening to Mom's guitar-shredding-hair-bands playlist. "If this is meant to be, it's meant to be. I'm tired of waiting. This is my dream and it will only come true if I do something about it—now!"

"Woo-hoo!" shouted all my friends.

"Rock on!" added Mom.

And then the van got sort of quiet.

"So, uh, what exactly are you gonna do, now, Jimmy?" asked Chris.

I yanked back on the sliding door handle. "I'm going to go inside and see if they accept walk-ins."

"And if they don't?"

"I'm going to camp out in their lobby until they do!"

Actually, camping in an office building would be awesome. You'd have heat and air conditioning. You wouldn't have to forage for food, just find the cafeteria or snack machines. And forget digging a latrine. It's the kind of camping even Alvin Ho from the book *Alvin Ho: Allergic to Camping, Hiking, and Other Natural Disasters* could enjoy.

Anyway, I climbed out of the van. My friends tumbled out after me.

Mom and Dad were eager to join the parade, too. I held up my hand.

"Um, you guys, if you don't mind, can you just sort of wait out here in the parking lot?"

"Huh?" Mom and Dad both said at the same time.

"My dream is to build a book company for *kids* that's run by *kids*. Bringing in my parents is kind of, you know, 'off message.'"

"Sure, sure," said Dad. "We'll wait out here."

My friends and I headed into the office building, toting a laptop computer, a file folder full of story ideas, and a cardboard tube stuffed with rolled-up sketches. We were carrying my dream!

Of all the venture capital firms and banks I'd visited on my quest, this one was the most incredibly amazing of them all. There were grown-up toys everywhere. A trampoline. A slide from the second story to the first. A basketball hoop. A mountain of Lego. Foosball, ping-pong, and billiards tables. Nap pods. There were even sleek Razor scooters you could ride up and down the halls.

The offices of Yingerlinger Enterprises also had the one thing I was looking for.

A reception desk!

Chapter 52

The Gatekeepers

This was it. It was now or never, do or die, and a dozen other sports clichés.

"Um, excuse me, sir," I said to the guy sitting behind the desk, which was kind of shaped like a bean you'd find on top of your chili dog.

"Yes?" The guy was smiling and wearing a super-cool head-mike–earphone combo. "May I help you?"

"Uh, yeah. I'm Jimmy."

The guy stopped tapping his keyboard and held out his hand. "Hello, Jimmy. I'm Guenther."

We shook.

"And, uh, these are my friends," I said, jabbing a thumb over my shoulder.

"Hello, Jimmy's friends," said Guenther.

"We're here to see Mr. and Mrs. Y."

"Why?"

"That's right."

"Excuse me?"

"The Ys are who I'm here to see."

"Why?"

"Yes. Mr. and Mrs."

Guenther sighed. "For what?"

"Oh, I have a great idea for a new company. But I don't have an appointment."

"Oh, that's okay," said Guenther. "Walk-ins are always welcome."

My eyes grew wide. "Really?" I couldn't believe my luck! "You guys will see anybody? You'll listen to any idea?"

"Company policy. Mr. and Mrs. Yingerlinger always say, 'We never know when the next big new idea is going to waltz through our front door.' Therefore, I have to warmly welcome any and all crackpots, nutjobs, and whackaloons—no matter their age."

Guenther smiled and blinked at me. A lot.

"Would you children like some milk and cookies?" he asked.

"No," I said. "We want to pitch our idea to Mr. and Mrs. Y!"

"Of course you do. So do half the high-tech wizards in Silicon Valley. But before you kids can even think about meeting the Yingerlingers, you have to pass through the Unsolicited Ideas Screeners."

He tapped a key. A number scrolled out of one of those "take a number" red plastic ticket dispensers they have at the deli counter in the supermarket.

So…

Three hours later, we were finally ushered into a conference room. Six bleary-eyed executives were seated on the other side of the table. They looked like they'd been smelling bad cheese all day.

"Um, where should we hook up the laptop?" asked Kenny. "We have a PowerPoint—"

"No," moaned one of the execs. "Not another PowerPoint!"

"We have diagrams and junk," said Rafe.

"No!" all the execs wailed. "No more slides! No more charts! No more diagrams! Just pitch us your idea."

All my friends turned to look at me.

I gulped. Mopped the sweat off my forehead with the tip of my scarf.

"You can do this, Jimmy," whispered Maxine.

"There is no try," said Chris. "Only do!"

Then all my buds started a low-volume chant. "Jim-my, Jim-my, Jim-my…"

I took in a deep breath.

I was ready to pitch as if it were the last inning of the last game of the World Series and we needed one more out to win!

Chapter 53

Dream Time

"First of all," I said, "thank you for your time…"

"Speaking of time," said a lady on the other side of the conference table as she flipped over an hour-glass egg timer. "You've got two minutes."

"My name is Jimmy," I said quickly. "And these are my friends."

Everybody waved. Quickly. The execs rolled their eyes.

"We have a dream," I said, remembering that guy in the wheelchair, the one who refused to give up no matter what obstacle he bumped into. "We want to start a book company for kids that's run by kids."

Rafe rolled out the floor plan.

"It'd be a super-fun place to work because we'd

only make books that were super-fun to read. Why? Because I believe a kid who reads is a kid who can succeed. I want to make reading fun for kids— through stories and voices that speak to them and expand their world. And I want to make more books available to more kids—through teacher scholar-ships, bookstore funding, school library support, and book donations."

"Um, is this a company or a charity?" asked a guy on the other side of the table.

"Both!" I answered. "And we've got to reach out to parents, too. Because I really think it's every adult's responsibility to get books into kids' hands and into kids' lives."

"What kind of books?" asked the lady.

"The kind kids can't put down. Maybe a story about an artistic kid in middle school having the worst years of his life because he's a round peg in a square hole. I want to do a story about a family of treasure hunters. And one about a kid in a wheel-chair who wants to be the world's funniest stand-up comic, even though he doesn't exactly fit the job description."

I opened my idea folder and dumped the papers on the table.

"I want to write about a house full of robots and a public school superhero and a mouse with a big vocabulary and an even bigger heart and two guys named Pottymouth and Stoopid . . ."

The lady raised both eyebrows. "The mouse has these two guys?"

"No. Sorry. I have so many ideas they sometimes come out in a jumble. Ideas that, together, we can turn into books that kids will love."

"But don't take Jimmy's word for it," said Chris Grabbetts (who could probably write commercials for late-night TV). "Listen to this unsolicited testimonial from his next-door neighbor, Maddie."

Chris flipped our laptop around and tapped the Play button.

A video clip filled the screen.

"Hi! My name is Maddie and Jimmy's books are the best."

The lady across the table took off her glasses. Squinted at the screen.

"Every time I read a book that Jimmy wrote,"

Maddie continued, "I say, 'Hey, Jimmy—please give me another book!'"

Now the lady was staring at me.

Hard.

Chapter 54

Surprise, Surprise

"You're that Jimmy?" asked the lady, tilting her head sort of sideways, I guess so she could gawk at me better.

"Um, yes, ma'am," I said. "Maddie's my next-door neighbor. She doesn't get out much on account of—"

"I know all about Maddie," said the lady, smiling at me warmly. "She's my niece. My *favorite* niece. You're the boy who brings her books from the library and gives her the ones you make up yourself?"

I nodded. "Yes, ma'am."

She turned to the other adults on her side of the table. "You guys? We need to bump this upstairs. Immediately. I have never seen Maddie happier than when she's reading one of Jimmy's books."

One of the guys at the table started fiddling with a calendar app on his tablet computer.

"The Ys have a fifteen-minute gap in their schedule. We could sandwich Jimmy in between their private speedboat lessons and their bull-riding event at the company rodeo this afternoon."

"That's today?" said another one of the execs, snapping his fingers. "I forgot to pack my chaps."

"Never mind," said Maddie's aunt. "Come on, Jimmy, we're going upstairs to the bird's nest."

"Huh?"

"That's what Mr. and Mrs. Yingerlinger call their office."

"Right now?"

"Yes. Unless, for some reason, you want to keep on waiting for your dream to come true?"

"No, ma'am! Come on, guys!"

Maddie's aunt held up her hand. "Your friends can't come with you, Jimmy."

"Huh?"

"This is *your* dream, correct?"

"Yes, but these guys all helped me so much…"

"Sorry. Mr. and Mrs. Yingerlinger only wish to directly interface with primary dreamers."

I turned to face my friends.

"Go for it," said Hailey.

"Do it, dude!" said Kenny.

"It seems to be the wise and prudent move," added Pierce.

And then everybody started chanting again,

only this time it was louder than a murmur.

"Jim-my, Jim-my, Jim-my!"

"Okay," I said to Maddie's aunt. "Take me up to the bird's nest!"

"Good luck, Jimmy!" shouted Maxine.

I grabbed the blueprints and my idea folder and headed for the door with Maddie's aunt.

"Don't forget to tell them about the bowling alley!" shouted Chris. "And the free nachos at the snack bar."

"Huh?" said a confused Kenny.

"Dude, who wants to go bowling if there aren't any nachos at the snack bar?"

That made me smile.

Well, as much as anything could make me smile with five thousand butterflies dancing the nae nae in my stomach.

Chapter 55

Y Not?

I entered an office filled with blindingly bright light because the fifteen-foot walls and ceiling were made entirely out of glass.

Even the window frames were made out of glass. The office was perched on top of the building's roof. It felt like an air-conditioned hothouse for flowers. I noticed several wacky sculptures of birds—like the guy on *Sesame Street*, only goofier.

"Welcome to the bird's nest," whispered Maddie's aunt. "Please remove your shoes."

I did.

"This is where I have to say good-bye," whispered Maddie's aunt.

"What?"

"It's your idea, Jimmy. You have to sell them on it—all by yourself."

She left. I gulped. Then I padded across the thick carpet in my stocking feet.

Mr. and Mrs. Yingerlinger, the bazillionaires, weren't sitting behind a big important desk. They were sprawled out in a pile of beanbag chairs slurping Lucky Charms out of cereal bowls with Muppet faces painted on the sides. They were both extremely young. Well, younger than my parents, anyway. And neither one was wearing a business suit. In fact, they were both wearing pajamas.

"What is it?" asked Mr. Yingerlinger.

"Who are you?" asked Mrs. Yingerlinger.

"Um, my name is, uh, Jimmy. And I just pitched an idea to your employees in the room where people go if, you know, they have ideas."

"And they sent you up here, straightaway?" said Mr. Yingerlinger, standing up and plucking a few

stray marshmallow moons off his pj's. "Oooh. This must be a fantastic idea, Jimmy!"

"We love those the most," said Mrs. Y, climbing out of the beanbag heap.

"But you know," said Mr. Y, "we're not just interested in fantastic *ideas*."

"Oh, no," said Mrs. Y. "We're just as interested in the fascinating *people* behind the fantastic ideas!"

"Fascinating people who can become fantastic partners," added Mr. Y.

"So, tell us, Jimmy," said Mrs. Y, "do you believe in your idea? Really, truly believe in it?"

"Or," said Mr. Y, "is this just a get-rich-quick scheme? An app that makes your phone burp or fart or a game involving exploding fruit?"

"No, sir," I said, pulling out Rafe's latest design for the book company. "It's not a scheme to make me rich. In fact, I'm really not all that interested in making money."

"Really?" said Mrs. Y skeptically.

"No, ma'am. I want to make books that make kids want to read more books. See, I love reading. Every time I finish a good book I want to find another one just as good. I want to do that for other kids. Whenever a kid finishes a book from the Laugh Out Loud Book Company, I want them to say, 'Wow! Give me another one!' But I'm a kid…"

"We noticed that," said Mrs. Y.

"I don't have the money to make my dream come true. I need your help. Can you guys be my financial angels? I think that's the term for it. My friend Hailey taught it to me."

Mr. and Mrs. Y looked at each other. Nodded.

"Why not!" they both said.

"Okay," I said. "Well, thanks for your time. I'll leave now..."

"Whoa," said Mrs. Y. "Where do you think you're going?"

"We're saying yes, Jimmy!" said Mr. Y.

I vaguely remember my heart stopped beating.

"You're really going to give me the money?" I asked.

"We sure are!" said Mr. Y. "Why not?"

"We're all in!" added his wife. "We love the idea of a book company for kids that's started by a kid and run by kids. It's outrageous. It's bold. It's a moon shot! There's nothing else like it."

"We love your company, Jimmy," said Mr. Y. "We love books! We love you! We love JIMMY Books."

Just then all my friends came crashing into the bird's nest cheering and chanting, "Jimmy! Jimmy! Jimmy!"

"But, um, the name of the company is Laugh Out Loud," I shouted over all the noise.

"Nah," said Mr. Y. "Having fun reading is too

important. We need to name the company after you, Jimmy."

I smiled at the Ys as my friends hugged each other and patted me on the back. My grin was so wide it hurt my face. We did it!

And that's how it all got started.

That's how the book company got its name, too.

My investors insisted. It was what they called a deal-breaker.

My name had to be on the cover of every book we published so I'd never, *ever* forget the promise I was personally making to each and every one of my readers: *Read this book and I guarantee you'll like it so much you'll want to read another one!*

Chapter 56

Back to School

The next day, I headed back to school, walking on air.

My dream was going to come true. The Yingerlingers would construct my amazingly fantastical idea for a book company on their property up in Marin County! Mom, Dad, Quixote, and I would be moving up there. My 'rents would have grown-up jobs in accounting and the legal department (none of my friends wanted those—not even Pierce). Most of my buds would be moving to

Marin County because I needed them to help me at JIMMY Books.

The Yingerlingers were going to build us a brand-new school on their property, too—because we had to keep learning stuff so we could keep coming up with new ideas for books.

My head was swimming with new ideas that could become books floating along on our lazy river and water slide assembly lines.

Unfortunately, my head should've been swimming with ideas for an extemporaneous speech. Because the second the bell rang, Mrs. Delvecchio once again declared, "All right, class, kindly put your books away. I'm waiting. Still waiting. Good. Today, we are going to, once more, continue our exploration of English and the power of words with another five-minute extemporaneous speech."

Then she turned to me.

"James?"

Uh-oh. Big trouble.

"Remember the last time I called on you?"

"Yes, ma'am."

"Well, this is it. Your final chance to avoid an F in English."

I stood up.

"You have five minutes, James. Go!"

I blasted off like a rocket!

"Guys, today I'd like to talk to you about my dream. I am going to start a book company for kids that's run by kids who know exactly what other kids want to read! We're going to make reading fun for kids because the more something is fun, the more of it gets done! It will be the most incredible book company in the entire world. Our books will take kids on exciting adventures! We'll open their eyes to whole new worlds and new ways of looking at things! My book company will have a river flowing through it—a river filled with floating books. We'll have a Ferris wheel instead of a freight elevator, too! Why? Because Ferris wheels are more fun! And all the employees will ride hoverboards. Real hoverboards. The kind without any wheels! They'll just float above the floor, the way a good book makes us float above the humdrum world!"

Yep, I gave a very rousing five-minute speech.

The exact same rousing speech I'd given the first time.

Which made Mrs. Delvecchio furious.

"As I told you the last time you related your ludicrous dream, James, in my classroom, an extemporaneous talk must be based on facts. It cannot be fiction."

"It's not fiction, Mrs. Delvecchio," I announced. "It's real. Yingerlinger Enterprises, the billionaire investors, are helping me launch JIMMY Books!"

I showed her the headline in the *Wall Street Journal,* a business newspaper that's big with grown-ups.

The kids in the class went absolutely nuts.

Mrs. Delvecchio's jaw dropped—to the floor.

Literally. Don't worry, the janitor cleaned it up.

Kidding.

(Or maybe I just came up with a new idea for another book!)

Chapter 57

Welcome to JIMMY Books!

So JIMMY Books officially opened six months after my first meeting with Mr. and Mrs. Y.

The factory is super-incredibly amazing. I think it cost like several kazillion dollars to build, but like the Yingerlingers always say, "most moon shots do." Hey, when you reach for the stars, if you fail, at least you land on a cloud.

Mostly kids work at JIMMY. In the idea department, the art department, the writing arena, the editing den, the proofreading porch—all over the place.

We have a couple of adults (Mom, Dad, and Maddie's aunt Amy) doing the stuff grown-ups do better than kids. You know—taxes, contracts, unclogging any clogged sinks or toilets.

Sure, we still go to school, but we have some amazing textbooks!

So guess what? That big dream I had? It came true!

Hey, maybe yours can, too! Just never, ever, ever give up!

Chapter 58

The Best Part of My Dream?

People often ask me, "Hey, Jimmy, what's the best part about running your own book company?"

Easy. The books! The stories. So many stories!

And so many more to come. (You've seen my idea folder. That thing is humongous!)

Middle School (which, wow, was turned into a movie!), *I Funny, House of Robots, Treasure Hunters, Jacky Ha-Ha, Word of Mouse, Pottymouth and Stoopid, Kenny Wright: Superhero*...even this one: *Laugh Out Loud.*

When you see my name on the cover, I guarantee it'll be a fun read or my name isn't Jimmy!

Epilogue

Jimmy's Who's Who List

So I guess by now you've probably figured out that some of the characters in this book went on to become characters in other JIMMY books.

Writing teachers always say, "Write what you know." Well, I expanded that a little to "write WHO you know, too!"

- **Madison,** my next-door neighbor, became **Maddie** in *House of Robots*. Her little brother, **Sammy,** came with her!

- **Chris Grabbetts** became one of my favorite coauthors. The guy's so prolific, these days he writes under TWO different pen names!
- **Raphael (Rafe) Katchadopoulos** turned into **Rafe Khatachadorian** in our Middle School series.
- **Maxine Peterman** is another one of my top coauthors and the reason I called the main character in *Maximum Ride* **Max**!
- **My dad,** the illustrator, became Maddie and Sam's father in *House of Robots*.
- **My mom's band** inspired the Pretty Awful rock band in *House of Robots*.
- **Mr. Quackenberry** turned into all the dream-crushers in all my books.
- My brainiac buddy **Pierce** morphed into Jamie Grimm's brainiac buddy **Pierce** in the I Funny books.
- **Hailey,** the girl with mice in her garage, became **Hailey** in *Word of Mouse*. The blue mouse she saw in her garage came along, too!
- **Kenny Wilson** became **Kenny,** the hero of *Kenny Wright: Superhero*.

- My imaginary aliens inspired me to create **Daniel X,** the alien hunter.
- The gutsy **guy in the wheelchair** led me to **Jamie Grimm** and the I Funny books.
- Don't tell her, but **Mrs. Delvecchio** became **the Dragon Lady** in *Middle School: The Worst Years of My Life*.
- Bickering twins **Bob and Abby Kipplemeyer** inspired **Bick and Beck Kidd** in the Treasure Hunters series.
- Yep, **Tailspin Tommy Kipplemeyer** turned into *Tailspin Tommy Kidd,* too!
- **Ms. Muenk, the English teacher,** inspired the character **Mrs. O'Mara** in *Jacky Ha-Ha*.
- The **robotic bankers** really did give me the idea for *House of Robots*!
- **Money Man,** my imaginary superhero, grew into **Stainlezz Steel** in *Kenny Wright: Superhero*.
- **Mr. and Mrs. Yingerlinger?** They became themselves in this book! Hey, why not?

**TURN THE PAGE
FOR A SNEAK PEEK AT**

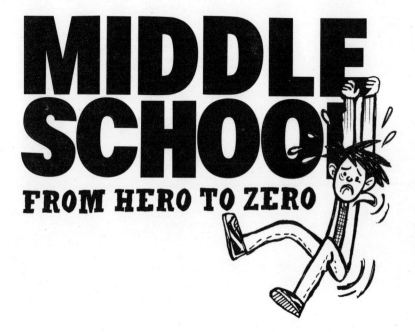

AVAILABLE JULY 2018

CHAPTER 1

PACKING UP

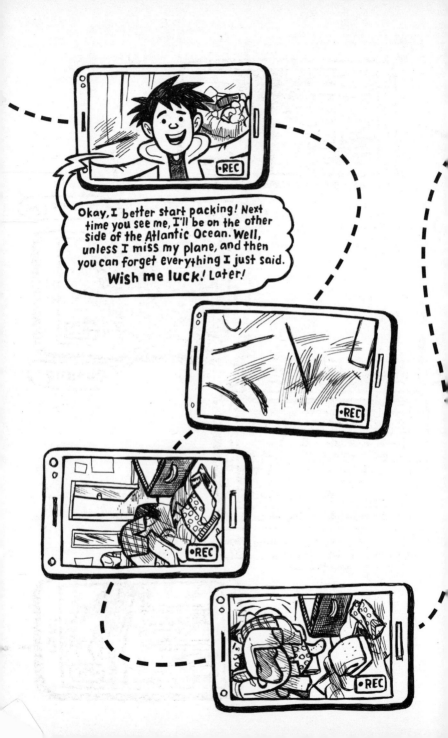

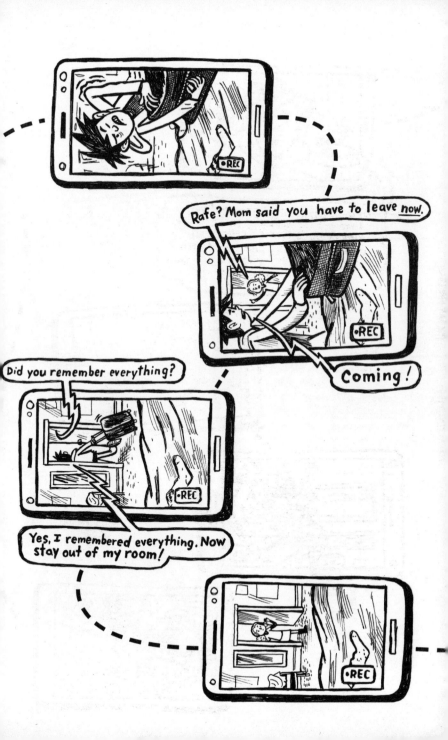

CHAPTER 2

TIME TO GO

At the airport, everything was crazy. There were kids and parents and chaperones trying to find each other, plus half a zillion other people, all traveling in half a zillion other directions.

And then there was a little room where we could all finally stop and gather up for our big good-byes before I had to find the other kids. It was definitely insane, but I could actually start to see the adventure I had been imagining.

"Excited?" Grandma asked me.

"Yep," I said, but honestly, I was kind of nervous, too.

"You sure you have everything?" Mom asked me.

"Yep," I said, even though I had this weird feeling I was forgetting something.

"Are you *really* sure you have everything?" Georgia asked, in that annoying way where you know she's not *really* asking a question. Then she held up the phone Grandma was lending me for the trip with a really smug smile.

"Where'd you get that?" I asked her.

"It was sitting on your bed while you were walking out the front door, genius," she said.

"I told you to stay out of my room," I said, and grabbed it back.

When it comes to snooping, my sister has superpowers. And she was definitely going to do some supersnooping while I was in London. That's why I'd spent the last week blowing my nose and leaving all the used Kleenex in my desk and dresser drawers. There was also some mega-realistic plastic dog puke on my closet floor, and a note under my mattress that said, "STOP SNOOPING OR DIE!"

But that was it. I couldn't worry about Georgia anymore. It was time to go. Mrs. Stricker was yelling at the parents to say good-bye so we could all get ready to hop into the security line, which looked about two miles long.

"All right, off you go," Mom said, and then walked me a little closer. When it comes to saying good-bye, Mom always likes a little time alone with me. I kind of like it, too.

"This is so exciting. Your first time out of the country without me!" she said. "And who would've thought you'd turn into such an international jetsetter? I thought Australia was exciting enough, what with the surfing and drop bears and the bunyip adventure, which I would personally rather forget." She stopped, embarrassed.

She was rambling about my last trip abroad—I won a school art competition and the prize was a free trip to the Land Down Under. Things didn't turn out so well, but I was glad I had the chance to go.

Even if it did end in disaster.

"You're going to have a great trip, sweetheart," Mom finished.

"Yeah…" I said. "I guess so."

"You guess?" Mom said.

"Well…"

"What is it?" she said.

She can always tell when I'm feeling weird about something. And this wasn't the kind of weird I wanted to put in a video, where everyone would hear about it. But I could tell Mom, even if it came out a little awkward.

See, this was supposed to be some great thing, right? I was really lucky to go somewhere as crazy exciting as London. (Grandma helped out and got her friends to buy about twenty thousand rolls of wrapping paper in our school fund-raiser, and I got a scholarship, thanks to Ms. Donatello.)

But here's the problem: the only real friends I had were staying back in Hills Village, on the wrong side of a pretty huge ocean. That included Flip Savage, the funniest kid I've ever known, and Junior, my dog and best non-human friend.

In other words, I was on my own for this trip. *Totally friend-free*. Which was like going back to the bad old days at Hills Village Middle School, when I was about as popular as Mystery Meat Monday in the cafeteria.

"It's just…I don't have any friends on this trip," I told Mom.

"What about Jeanne Galletta?" Mom asked.

"Jeanne doesn't count," I said. "She's really nice, but it's not like we're actually friends."

I probably (definitely) wasn't supposed to like Jeanne as much as I did. But try telling that to my brain. I just couldn't help it.

Right now, Jeanne was standing with the rest of the kids along with her stupid perfect boyfriend, Jared McCall, who I am NOT jealous of. It's just that Jared's so good at everything, you kind of want to stick his head in a toilet sometimes.

"Well, I see at least one girl looking your way, Rafe. I think you might be more popular with the ladies than you realize."

"Don't say *ladies*," I said. "And besides, you're my mom. You have to say that stuff."

"How about Ms. Donatello?" Mom said. "You like her, don't you?"

"Sure," I said. "For a teacher. But that doesn't really count."

"Well, here's an idea. Why don't you try making a few *new* friends?" Mom asked me.

That one was harder to answer. I mean, everyone in middle school already knew me, and it wasn't like I'd been sitting on all the good parts of my personality so I could bust them out now and start winning popularity contests. I pretty much knew by now who my friends were and *who wouldn't be caught dead talking to me*.

I didn't know if Mom would understand all that, but I'll bet you do, right?

"I guess," I mumbled, which was easier than telling her everything I just told you.

"It can't hurt to be friendly," Mom said. "I

wouldn't want you to spend the whole trip alone with that sketchbook of yours."

She had a point. I did bring my sketchbook, for sure. I love to draw, including my Loozer comics, which you may already know about. You'll definitely see some more of those later.

"Now, you better go or Mrs. Stricker is going to leave without you," she said.

Mrs. Stricker is the principal of Hills Village Middle School. She also happens to hate the ground I walk on. Right now, she was evil-eyeing me like I was holding up the whole airport.

"Sorry, Ida," Mom called out to her. "He's coming!"

"Mmglrrr," Mrs. Stricker mumbled, which I think was something about *should have left without him.* But I couldn't be sure.

"Bon voyage, sweetie!" Mom said, and gave me one more quick hug for luck. "I love you. And remember what I said."

"I will," I told her.

And I would.

I'd remember every word…just as soon as I got busy being the *least* popular kid on that whole trip.

Hey, it's a tough job, but someone has to do it.